SPECTRUM 4

Spectrum 1996
Call for Entries Poster
Sculpture & concept: **BILL NELSON**
art director/designer: Arnie Fenner
medium: mixed media construction
size: various

*The Best
In Contemporary
Fantastic Art*

Spectrum 4

edited by
Cathy & Arnie Fenner
with Jim Loehr

UNDER
WOOD
BOOKS

For information on limited edition fine art prints by James Gurney, James Christensen, and Scott Gustafson
call The Greenwich Workshop at 1-800-243-4246.

Trade Softcover Edition ISBN 1-887424-28-8
Hardcover Edition ISBN 1-887424-29-6
10 9 8 7 6 5 4 3 2 1

. Special thanks to Bill Nelson, Cortez Wells, Bud Plant, James Gurney, and Rick Berry for their continued support and enthusiasm. And special thanks to Joseph DeVito for sculpting Spectrum's gold, silver, and grand master awards.

Dedicated to the "boys"
BOB FENNER & ARLO BURNETT

*A day doesn't pass
when we're not reminded of how fortunate we are.*

STEVE HOLLAND
*It is with sadness we note the passing of Steve Holland [1925—1997]. Artist, athlete, and actor (he played "Flash Gordon"
in the short-lived 1950s TV series), Mr. Holland was the premiere model for book jacket artists for nearly 50 years.
Perhaps best known as the model for all of James Bama's "Doc Savage" paintings, Mr. Holland's dramatic skills were utilized
on thousands of covers in all genres, including westerns, SF, and romance. His talent and professionalism will be missed.*

Published by UNDERWOOD BOOKS, P.O. BOX 1609, GRASS VALLEY, CA 95945
TIM UNDERWOOD / PUBLISHER

Contents

EDITOR'S MESSAGE

Cathy Fenner & Arnie Fenner
with Jim Loehr

Arnie & Cathy Fenner/Photograph by Lainey Koepke

One would think that after having three previous *Spectrum* competitions and annuals under our belts we would have the system down to a science and that the fourth one would hum along like a well-oiled machine. While that's a nice thought, the reality is that each *Spectrum* is a different beast with its own set of rewards and difficulties.

One of the things we've learned is that it doesn't get easier. As we've stated several times in the past, we don't have corporate sponsors or a dues-paying membership, we don't have a magazine or selection of spin-off products to help off-set finances and keep our name out in the marketplace. *Spectrum* is organized and compiled and worried over by just the three directors: its continuance is made possible by the members of the creative community that participates in the competition, support from both those who are selected for inclusion in the annual along with those who disappointingly are not. Alternately exhilarating and frustrating, each year has its own unique set of hurdles to overcome.

Conversations with readers and artists and critics over the previous year have brought up an interesting question: Should *Spectrum* try to elevate the form of fantastic art, to transcend the constrictions of genre, or should it embrace and celebrate the icons and recognized symbols of sf, fantasy, and horror?

After very little thought (and ignoring the fact that the contents of each book is determined by the artists and the juries,) we believe that *Spectrum* should do both.

In recent years corporations around the country have bought into the concept of "mission statements," nice concise *Dilbert*-flavored lists of obvious purpose and vague goals. Why a company believes it's a great revelation to spell out what everybody knows already is anybody's guess. ("We want to make more money and we want to make customers sufficiently happy to spend more money on our stuff"—forget all the fairytales tossed in about caring about the community and their employees; that's just p.r. to keep the crowds docile until the time is right to screw them.) Perhaps coming up with buzz-words and restating the obvious have become art-forms deserving of their own annuals.

But we'll play along (just this once) and use the corporate jargon to more completely answer the question posed above. Our "mission statement" is quite simple: this series will continue to *reflect* and showcase the best of what is being created each year in the field of fantastic art, featuring both examples that fit the traditional confines of genre and those that transcend it.

By its very nature fantastic art is vast and all encompassing: Its perimeters (if there are any) are determined by the practitioners and the viewers. The obvious is as valid a contribution to the form as is the subtle (and vice-versa.) To attempt to define the parameters of fantastic art through *Spectrum* would defeat its purpose: This is a celebration of diversity, a festival of the imagination, and all sensibilities are welcome with talent as the unifying factor. If *Spectrum* in some way helps to establish a standard of excellence for the fantastic arts then no small recognition is due the creative community that has annually supported this endeavor.

Our sincerest thanks once again to the overworked jury, our sympathetic advisors, the readers, and the artists and companies that have made *Spectrum 4*—this celebration—possible!

THE JURY

Gary Kelley
artist

Photograph by Bill Witt

Sue Ann Harkey
art director:
Wizards
of the Coast

Portrait by Geof Darrow/colored by Corey Macourek

Maria Carbado
designer/
art director

Vincent DiFate
artist/President:
The Society
of Illustrators

Photograph by Murray Tinkelman

Bud Plant
publisher/illustration historian

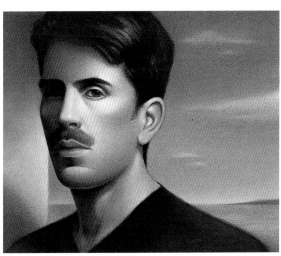

Self portrait by Vern Dufford

Vern Dufford
senior designer/Hallmark Cards

GRAND MASTER AWARD

LEO & DIANE DILLON

Born on opposite coasts in the same month and year, it was probably preordained that Leo Dillon and Diane Sorber would be brought together at the Parsons School of Design in New York City in 1953. Both attracted to and intimidated by each other's talent and determination, their collaborations on class assignments led to a romantic relationship that culminated in their marriage after graduation in 1957. Rather than pursue separate careers and compete with each other for assignments they decided to fuse their personalities into a single and singular artistic vision that is unique in the history of fantastic art. For over 40 years Leo and Diane Dillon have melded their distinctive skills successfully and amazingly into a third entity that even they refer to in conversations as "the artist."

The Dillons have never confined themselves to any particular medium or subject matter. Examining the body of their work reveals art employing pastels, acrylics, stencils, typography, woodcut, pochoir, and various sorts of sculpture for every type of client, from the most innocent books for children to the most volatile of political tracts. (It's been said that their graphic raised-fist cover for *The Goddam White Man* by David Lytton was anonymously copied to become the symbol of the Black Power movement of the 1960s.) Their covers for the *Ace Science Fiction Specials* and numerous books by Harlan Ellison garnered them the Hugo Award for Best Artists in 1971, while their art for *Why Mosquitoes Buzz in People's Ears* and *Ashanti to Zulu* earned them the prestigious Caldecott Medal in 1976 and 1977. They were further honored by the Society of Illustrators in 1976 with the Hamilton King Award for excellence in illustration and the Correta Scott King Award in 1990 for their paintings for *Aida* and the C.S.K. Honor for the art for *Her Stories: African American Folk Stories* in 1996. The Dillons have taught at the School of Visual Arts, Diane is a past president of the Graphic Artists Guild, and they have exhibited their work in galleries and museums around the globe. Their son Lee, a fine artist in his own right, has participated in their collaborative world, contributing stunning sculpted frames and dimensional additions to their art for *Pish, Posh, Said Hieronymus Bosch* and *The Chronicles of Narnia* series. Ballantine Books published *The Art of Leo & Diane Dillon* (their only collection to date) in 1981.

Leo and Diane don't really talk about their art or the philosophies and symbolism expressed in it too much. They just *create*, in a flurry of excitement and with a sense of urgency that ignores deadline constraints and client preconceptions. A willingness to be surprised (and delighted) is a prerequisite of working with the Dillons.

Some critics have said that their refusal to lock themselves into a particular style or technique has prevented the Dillons from gaining the public's "brand-name" recognition that they might have otherwise achieved. But that viewpoint ignores the obvious constant that is *always* evident in their work:

Excellence.

And it is that excellence, and the *quest* for excellence, that makes Leo and Diane Dillon extraordinarily significant in the august history of fantastic art. Experiencing their work, for the first or the hundredth time, proves the point.

both born in March, 1933

SPECTRUM

THE YEAR IN REVIEW BY ARNIE FENNER

▼

It was the best of times, it was the worst of times—at least, 1996 might have seemed that way to observers and aficionados of the fantastic arts. An infinite array of products and projects by an equally diverse range of creatives and publishers vied for consumers' attention (and disposable income). But that vast quantity of works had something of an oddly schizophrenic effect, pleasing some while confusing or frustrating or alienating others.

There were artistic gems that were lauded and revered and others that were sadly ignored; illustrative drek that raked in enormous praise and profits as works in a similar vein were over-zealously trashed; compilations of stunning art that showcased worthy talents sat side-by-side with collections that perhaps shouldn't have been published at

John Berkey's sophisticated artwork helped Science Fiction Age *and* Realms of Fantasy *assume the mantle left by* Omni's *departure for cyberspace.*

all—just as enormous bodies of historically significant works and their creators remained unjustly obscure; publishers came and publishers went, most with a whimper, not a bang; museums and galleries and auctions successfully showed again that fantastic art is a part of the mass consciousness with international appeal while genre conventions (with exceptions) continued to treat their "art shows" and participants with an almost benign contempt; and com-

puters...well, let's just say that it's a wonderful tool, but at times last year it appeared that the tail wagged the dog.

And when the dust settled and 1996 became just another memory for the scrapbook...it was another typical year.

With a few wrinkles.

ADVERTISING

▼

Last year I had briefly touched on the growing presence of computer-generated or computer-manipulated imagery in the advertising field. That presence seemed to become uncomfortably dominant during the past twelve months.

Situations that in the past could only be realized through traditional paintings or expensive photo shoots and hand-retouching were easily created cost-effectively with stock images and a variety of computer software and filters, often with amazing results. Morph people into animals, float houses in tornadoes, distort features, put a couch in orbit—think of it and there's a computer program and savvy artist that can bring it to reality. But the simple fact remains that the *artist* was and is the key to the success of a project: no software automatically composes a page creating harmony and balance. No computer has a magical eye for detail or the ability to distinguish what's important and what's not.

That the vast majority of film posters in 1996 were computer-enhanced or created wasn't a surprise: their effectiveness had more to do with the skill of the designers and art directors than with the tool used to create them.

But computer art (again with notable exceptions) still tends to be somewhat

cool and (dare I say it?) artificial. So, given that advertisers want to appeal to consumers in a personal manner ("We're your old friends: you can trust *us,*") it's not astonishing that in this digital age there was a quantity of traditionally-created art used for a broad range of clients through the months.

Rafal Olbinski's arresting work for the South Coast Repertory, Daniel Craig's poster for the New York City Opera's *HMS Pinafore*, Eric White's bizarre cover for Brown Lobster Tank's album "Tooth Smoke," and Bill Mayer's typically manic monster for Computer Associates Software were all standouts. John Rush, Tim Jessell, Jerry Lofaro, Anita Kunz, Jody Hewgill, Brad Holland, Eric Dinyer, Steven Adler, and C.F. Payne all produced exciting and memorable works.

EDITORIAL

◆

If you have an interest or a hobby there is undoubtedly some periodical that caters to it. But while there *always* have been science fiction and fantasy magazines, from both major publishers and small presses, 1996 seemed to be something of a lean year. Declining circulations and an aging reader demographic could buttress opinions that short f&sf, at least in a magazine format, had become more of a specialized niche market. Whether that's true or not is something for observers with an inside track to decide.

The sale of *Analog* and *Asimov's Science Fiction* to the Penny Press sent mini shockwaves throughout the community, especially in light of the knowledge that the buyer had little interest in either title and was primarily after the Dell line of puzzle magazines. The unexpected departure of Terri Czeczko as longtime art director left a question mark as to what will happen (at least artistically) to what were once the most popular fiction digests in the field. *Asimov's* sported nice covers by Wojtek Siudmak,

Kinuko Y. Craft, and Bob Eggleton while *Analog* featured notable pieces by George Krauter, Mark Salwowski, and Todd Lockwood.

The Magazine of Fantasy & Science Fiction, long considered the aristocrat of the digests, included beautiful covers by Barclay Shaw, Jill Bauman, and Bryn Barnard. Paul Lehr provided some stunning work to the semi-professional *Tomorrow SF* and *Worlds of Fantasy & Horror* was highlighted by the bright covers of Ian Miller and Douglas Beekman.

With *Omni's* disappearance from the traditional market, Sovereign Media's *Realms of Fantasy* and *Science Fiction Age* (both art directed by Stephen Vann) became the genre magazines with the highest newsstand profile. Printed in full color they showcased work by Chris Moore, John Berkey, Stephen Youll, David Beck, Richard Powers, Barclay Shaw, and Dean Morrissey among many others. Other smaller periodicals like *Interzone*, *Marion Zimmer Bradley's Fantasy Magazine*, *Lore*, and *Cemetery Dance* included work by a wide variety of talent.

The irreverent *Mad* was a forum for what they call their "usual gang of idiots," featuring excellent covers by Mark Frederickson, Joseph DeVito, and Richard Williams and interior work by such legendary creators as Mort Drucker, Angelo Torres and Jack Davis. And the outré Los Angeles gallery, Dark's Art Parlour, produced a magazine of the same name mixing fiction with the art of clients Eric Dinyer, K.D. Matheson, and Paul Winternitz.

Naturally fantastic art isn't limited to the genre magazines and crops up wonderfully in practically any title you might name. *Playboy*, of course, maintained it's position as *the place* to look for the best in both traditional and cutting-edge illustration. As art directed by

Wayne Barlowe's follow-up to his popular Barlowe's Guide to Extraterrestrials *focused on fantasy's popular characters.*

Tom Staebler, they published tremendous work by Wilson McLean, Robert Giusti, Kent Williams, and Brad Holland among many others. *Rolling Stone* included notable pieces by Anita Kunz and Gary Kelley, *The Atlantic Monthly* included typically wonderful work by C.F. Payne, *The National Geographic* was accented by John Gurche's dramatic oil paintings of prehistoric life, and Peter de Sève's art for *The New Yorker* (art directed by Françoise Mouly) was topnotch. Looking through everything from *Time* to *Esquire* to *Entertainment Weekly* to *Boys Life* would reveal affecting work by everyone from Don Ivan Punchatz to Tim O'Brian to Peter Kuper to Gary Baseman and beyond.

Magazines like *Communication Arts*, *How*, and *Step-By-Step Graphics* are invaluable to people interested in staying abreast of trends in illustration (available at most bookstores,) while those wanting to know more about the doings of the science fiction & fantasy field (including books, events, personalities, and periodicals) will be amply rewarded by the industry's monthly trade journal, *Locus* (P.O. Box 13305, Oakland, CA 94661. Sample issue: $5.00.)

BOOKS

•

Any and all art techniques and styles were evident in the book world throughout the year: photo-realistic works appeared spine-to-spine with "naive" covers, complex multi-layered computer images vied with stark graphic renderings for attention, the cool and sedate competed with punkish outrageousness. While insiders argued that SF, fantasy, and horror were in something of a slump (and the use of stock photos and fine art paintings for covers was more evident than ever before) it wasn't apparent when looking at some of the wonderful work appearing in (but not limited to) the fantastic field.

Mark Ryden's Daliesque matching covers for "Richard Bachman's" *The Regulators* and Stephen King's *Desperation* (both from Viking) were eerily complimented by Don Maitz's cover and in-

terior illustrations for the collector's edition of the latter (Donald M. Grant.) Barry Moser provided a memorable set of woodcuts for Joyce Carol Oates' *First Love* (Ecco), Chris Van Allsburg beautifully illustrated *A City in Winter* by Mark Helprin (Viking), and Gary Kelley's haunting art complimented Edgar Allan Poe's *Tales of Mystery & Imagination* (Harcourt Brace.) Bernie Fuchs' jacket for Ray Bradbury's *Quicker Than the Eye* was quietly touching, John Jude Palencar's covers for Warner Aspects' reissue of the books by Octavia Butler were truly extraordinary, Richard Bober's paintings for Gene Wolfe's Tor editions were lush masterworks, and Kinuko Y. Craft's jackets for the Ace editions of Patricia McKillip's books (like *Winter Rose*) harkened back to the Renaissance.

Michael Whelan was represented by a brace of paintings completed before he went on his commercial art sabbatical at the end of 1995, including covers for *Dreamfall* by Joan Vinge (Warner) and Melanie Rawn & co.'s *The Golden Key* (Daw.) Jackets by Tom Kidd for *The Waterborn* by J. Gregory Keyes (Del Rey,) Jim Burns for *Ancient Shores* by Jack McDevitt (Harper Prism,) Jody Lee for *Hunter's Death* by Michelle West (Daw,) and Mary GranPré for *Fair Peril* by Nancy Springer (Avon) were exceptional.

Frank Frazetta's new book featured a selection of his most recent artworks, but long-time fans were left wondering if a complete retrospective collection of the influential illustrator's paintings would ever appear.

A glance at the shelves revealed a breathtaking selection of jacket art by John Howe, Mel Odom, Simon Ng, Josh Kirby, Haydn Cornner, Gnemo, Stephen

Youll, Steve Crisp, John Ennis, Dorian Vallejo, Donato Giancola, Vincent Di-Fate, Bruce Jensen, Gary Ruddell, Stephen Hickman, John Bolton, Thomas

Alan Lee's luminous paintings for Rosemary Sutcliff's The Wanderings of Odysseus *added another highpoint to that English artist's brilliant career.*

Canty, Daniel Horne, and Peter de Sève to name only a very few. The list could easily go on for the next several pages.

Britain's Dragon's World, whose Paper Tiger imprint was for years the preeminent publisher of fantastic art collections, surprised the industry by closing shop and filing for bankruptcy. The assets of the company (but none of the debts or obligations) were taken over by Collins & Brown: their intentions for the inventory and the imprint itself remained unclear, but it was unlikely that any owed royalties would be paid to artists for their books. David Mattingly's collection, *Alternate Views, Alternate Universes*, was released just prior to the announcement in November.

FPG, traditionally a publisher of trading cards, seemed determined to fill the void, however, and began an aggressive fantasy art book program. Their initial releases included *Joe Jusko's Art of Edgar Rice Burroughs* and *Star Wars: The Art of Dave Dorman*, with collections by Keith Parkinson, Brom, and Boris, among others, scheduled to follow in '97.

Neurotica: The Darkest Art of J.K. Potter (Overlook) was a disquieting showcase for a unique talent—the fine art world would probably enthusiastically em-

brace his edgy, disturbing work if it was marketed to them. Morpheus International likewise produced books that appealed to readers beyond the conventions of genre including *River of Mirrors: The Fantastic Art of Judson Huss*, *H.R. Giger's Film Design*, and *Krüger Stones*, a hilariously demented selection of skewed "portraits" of the Rolling Stones by Sebastian Krüger.

Wayne D. Barlowe's *Barlowe's Guide to Fantasy* (Harper Prism) worked both as a forum for an influential artist and a handy guidebook to the more popular characters and creatures of the field. Brian Froud teamed again with Monty Python's Terry Jones for a humorous sequel to their *Lady Cottington's Pressed Fairy Book*, this time entitled *Strange Stains & Mysterious Smells* (Turner,) and NBM had an instant hit on their hands with Luis Royo's erotic collection, *Secrets*. Similarly, SQ Productions published a series of fantasy-flavored pin-up books, including *Crimson Embrace II*, *Jungle Tails*, and *Conan the Cruel* which featured drawings by Howard Chaykin, Joseph Linser, Joe Jusko, and Stephen Hickman among others. They also produced *Flesh & Fire: The Blas Gallego Sketchbook* and *Xotica: The Art of Estaban Maroto*. And the year wouldn't have been complete without *William Stout: 50 Convention Sketches* (Vol. 4 in '96, published by the artist each year for his appearance at the San Diego Comic Convention)—sophisticated art hiding behind a deceptive title.

Editors Clifford Ross and Karen Wilkin explored *The World of Edward Gorey* (Abrams) while Michael Sowa's art was the focus of *Sowa's Ark: An Enchanted Bestiary* (Chronicle Books.) *Mary Engelbreit: The Art and the Artist* (Andrews & McMeel) was an exhaustive career overview of the world's premiere illustrator of greeting cards, and *Myth, Magic, And Mystery: 100 Years of American Children's Book Illustration* (Roberts Rinehart) was a comprehensive companion to the touring museum show of the same name

featuring everyone from Dr. Seuss to Arthur Rackham. *Realms of Tolkien: Images of Middle Earth* (Harper Prism) beautifully transported readers through the art of such favorites as John Howe, Michael Kaluta, Alan Lee, and Stephen Hickman, among others, and Steltman's *Michael Parkes* was highlighted by the artist's latest sculptures and lithographs.

Grand Master Frank Frazetta's recent paintings (including many previously unpublished pieces) were collected in the perhaps pricey, simply titled *Frazetta* (Frazetta Prints.) Michael Whelan's horror works were gathered in his wonderfully ghoulish *Something In My Eye* poster book (Ziesing) while Vanguard produced a small treasure (5"x6") with *Marshall Arisman's Light Runners*.

And of course there was a marvelous selection of children's books that appealed to anyone with a love of fantastic art. *The Voyage of the Basset* by James Christenson, with Renwick St. James and Alan Dean Foster (Artisan/GW,) was an astonishing volume featuring a bewitching array of Christensen's minutely detailed drawings and paintings.

Alan Lee's mystical watercolors for *The Wanderings of Odysseus* by Rosemary Sutcliff (Delacourt) were a delight as was Kuniko Y. Craft's work for *Baba Yaga and Vasilisa the Brave* by Marianna Mayer and *Cupid and Psyche* by M. Charlotte Craft (both published by Morrow.) Scott Gustafson's art for *Nutcracker* by E.T.A. Hoffman (Ariel) was vibrant and Charles Santore's illustrations for *Snow White* (Park Lane) were engaging.

David Shannon continued to amaze with his art for *The Bunyans* by Audrey Wood (Scholastic,) Alan Vaës entertained with his tale of animated tools trying to make lunch, *29 Bump Street* (Turner,) and Lane Smith energetically illustrated Roald Dahl's *James and the Giant Peach* (Disney). *Wayne Anderson's Horrorble Book* (Dorling Kindersly) was spooky fun, Phil Parks revealed the secret of *Santa's Twin* by Dean Koontz (Harper Prism,) and Victor Lee answered the question *Where Did All the Dragons Go?* by Fay Robinson (Bridgewater.) Grennady Spirin, Leo and Diane Dillon, William Joyce, and Graeme Base (to name only a small fraction) produced memorable works all through the year.

There were books for animation fans (like *Tex Avery: The MGM Years, 1942-*

1955 [Turner] and *Alex Toth: By Design!* [Gold Medal],) how-to books (like the *Encyclopedia of Fantasy & Science Fiction Art Techniques* [Running Press],) and books reexamining the art of past masters (like *N.C. Wyeth: The collected Paintings, Illustrations & Murals* [Wings] or *Hannes Bok Drawings and Sketches* [Mugster].) The catalogs of Bud Plant Comic Art (P.O. Box 1689, Grass Valley, CA 95945) remained as *the best* resources for all manner of illustrated books, comics, and miscellaneous products.

COMICS

As I said in the opening, it was the best of times, it was the worst of times: nowhere was it more evident than in the world of comics in 1996. Still staggered by the collapse of the speculator's market, changes in distribution, comic shop failures, and attacks by pro-censorship zealots, alarmed readers and publishers and retailers discovered that the turbulent waters hadn't settled yet.

Diamond Comic Distributors, Inc. became the only major player in the direct market when they purchased competitor Capital City Distribution: Diamond's CEO Steve Geppi calmed some alternative publishers' fears by pledging to support the diversity of product that Capital was known for...which didn't prevent others from voicing concerns about there being only one major distributor of comics and related material when "in the old days" there had been almost a dozen.

Meanwhile, Marvel (who had upset the distribution applecart last year) tried to pull their company (and their stocks) out of a downward spiral by canceling titles, terminating staff, and reinventing their most popular characters, like The Fantastic Four and Captain America. It didn't work. Newspaper headlines in late December trumpeted Marvel's bankruptcy and detailed a nasty internal struggle for control of the

Steve Fastner and Rich Larson's sexy Demon Baby *exhibited a fine eye for design, attractive airbrush artwork, and a devilish (ahem!) sense of humor.*

very popular company and its future.

Image Comics, a creator-established publisher, had its own set of internal difficulties. Broadway Comics disappeared entirely, movies based on comic characters (like *Barb Wire*, *The Phantom*, and *Mars Attacks!*) tanked at the box office after strong starts, readers' tastes were routinely insulted (or pandered to) with a plethora of comic characters' butt-or-boob-shots, and everyone from the top on down felt the effects of a market slump in some way or another.

And yet...

And yet there was an eclectic, wondrous variety of comics and graphic novels published throughout the year.

DC Comics seemed to rise above the fray and went about the business of fearlessly publishing some of the most experimental titles in mainstream comics. They were confident enough to play with the concept of Batman in their 4-issue mini-series *Batman Black & White*. Quirky stories by Ted McKeever, Bruce Timm, Joe Kubert, Kent Williams, Simon Bisley (script by Neil Gaiman,) Bill Sienkiewicz, Brian Bolland, and Gary Gianni (script by Archie Goodwin) were all stunning in their execution and mood. The Man of Steel got an effective make-over in Ted McKeever's one-shot *Superman's Metropolis* (inspired by Fritz Lang's film, script by R.J.M. Lofficier and Roy Thomas.) And *all* of DC's characters had roles in the apocalyptic *Kingdom Come*, beautifully rendered by Alex Ross (quite intelligently written by Mark Waid.) Other art worthy of attention included Peter Kuper's *Vertigo Vérité*, various covers by Glenn Fabry, John Bolton, Tom Taggart, and Sean Phillips, Jon J. Muth's evocative *Farewell, Moonshadow*, and Teddy Kristiansen's creepy and effective drawings for the re-

vived *House of Secrets* dark fantasy series.

Kitchen Sink Press also made lemonade out of the field's economic lemons and produced a stack of exciting books. John Mueller's collected *Oink:*

Alex Ross' painted interiors and Mark Waid's script gave DC's Kingdom Come *4-issue mini-series an epic, mythic quality that was appealing to long-time fans and non-traditional comics readers alike.*

Heaven's Butcher and his covers for *The Crow: Wild Justice* were superb (as were Charlie Adlard's interiors for the latter title.) Erez Yakin's wordless dystopian allegory, *The Silent City*, was thoughtful and moving as was Matthew Coyles' art for *Registry of Death* (script by Peter Lamb.) *The Will Eisner Sketchbook* was a fascinating glimpse of the creative process by one of comics' true legends while the new issue (after nearly two years) of Mark Schultz's carefully-crafted *Xenozoic Tales* (#14) was a stunning showcase for a legend-in-the-making. Kitchen Sink's various Robert Crumb titles (like *Waiting For Food: Restaurant Placemat Drawings*,) their ongoing *Li'l Abner* compilation series by Al Capp and Frank Frazetta, and Steve Weiner's *100 Graphic Novels for Public Libraries* all exhibited a love for and commitment to the art form that was admirable.

Dark Horse Comics, too, published a stack of noteworthy comics during the year, mixing their line of licensed properties (like *Star Wars*™) with creator-owned titles. Mike Mignola's *Hellboy:*

Wake the Devil was brilliantly subtle and manic and scary and funny—all at the same time!—while Gary Gianni's *Silent as the Grave* back-up feature was a pure delight. Art Adams' *Monkeyman and O'Brien* was refreshingly nostalgic, *Barry*

The Greenwich Workshop produced a line of fanciful limited edition figurines (like the "Forest Fishrider" shown here) inspired by the paintings of James Christensen.

Windsor-Smith: Storyteller was an oversized forum for a 1970's icon, and Ricardo Delgado's *Age of Reptiles* was entertaining. *Harlan Ellison's Dream Corridor* returned with both a new edition and a compilation volume of the first 6 issues: featuring adaptations by Doug Wildey, Neal Adams, Craig Elliot, John K. Snyder III, and Heinrich Kipper (just to mention a few,) *HEDC* was (and is) a nonguilty pleasure. Steve Rude's *Nexus*, Paul Chadwick's ecologically-themed *Concrete: Think Like a Mountain*, and Arthur Suydam's various Frazetta-flavored *Tarzan* covers were all worth seeking out.

Bill Waterson's *Calvin & Hobbes* strips were published in two final collections, *There's Treasure Everywhere* and *It's a Magical World*, and Gary Larson's *The*

Far Side made a last appearance in the appropriately titled *The Last Chapter and Worse* (both from Andrews & McMeel.) *Comics, Comix & Graphic Novels* (Phaidon) by Roger Sabin was a compelling history of the art form, *The Comic Book Heroes* (Prima) by Will Jacobs and Gerard Jones was an intelligent examination of the field, and Digby Diehl's *Tales From the Crypt* (St. Martin's) was the definitive book about E.C. and its artists.

Fantagraphics Books' *Jim* by Jim Woodring and *Stripped* by Peter Kuper displayed excellent work on the cutting-edge as did Allen Spiegel Fine Arts with *Visions of Vespertina* by Greg Spalenka and Michelle Barnes. Other art of note included Jhonen Vasquez's *Johnny the Homicidal Maniac* (Slave Labor,) Frank Frazetta's, Ray Lago's, and Mark Texeira's work for the *Vampirella 25th Anniversary Special* (Harris,) Michael T. Gilbert's *Mr. Monster: His Books of Forbidden Knowledge* (Graphitti/Marlowe & Co.,) NBM's *Burne Hogarth's Tarzan* and *The Mercenary: Year 1000* by Vincente Segrelles, and the erotic *Demon Baby* (SQ) by Steve Fastner and Rich Larson. Miscellaneous covers and interiors by Greg Loudon, Ken Meyer, Jr., Marc Hempel, Rick Berry, Bill Stout, Bernie Wrightson, Michael Kaluta, Ashley Wood, Bill Sienkiewicz, Geof Darrow, Charles Burns, Dave Stevens, John Bolton, Milo Manara, Jeff Smith, Daniel Brereton, Alex Ross, Bill Wray, Simon Bisley, Brent Anderson, Miran Kim, and Kent Williams proved again that comics had a little bit of something for every one.

Except, of course, an objective, unbiased, responsible trade journal.

DIMENSIONAL
▲

There was something of a 3-D explosion in 1996 with almost an overabundance of noteworthy statues and sculptures and...cool *stuff.*

The Greenwich Workshop produced an exquisite line of finely-crafted figures based on the art of James Christensen as well as a pair of charmingly-carved children's chairs designed by Scott Gustafson in a limited edition.

Bowen Designs released a tremendous bust of Hellboy (designed by Mike Mignola/sculpted by Randy Bowen) and

Stephen Hickman's "Cthullu" statue (see *Spectrum 3*.) Hellboy was also the subject of an attractive model kit sculpted by Shawn Nagle for Polydata.

Graphitti Designs pulled out all the stops with their bronze Tarzan statue, sculpted by Joseph DeVito and designed by the late Burne Hogarth—the pure craftsmanship and care for details were truly awe-inspiring. Graphitti also produced the whimsical "Red Dragon" (designed by Jeff Smith/sculpted by Randy Bowen) from the *Bone* comics and "Groo Takes a Dip" (designed and sculpted by Sergio Aragonés.)

Clayburn Moore was busy in bronze, too, with his stunning "Princess" statue, inspired by Frazetta's *A Fighting Man of Mars* painting. His "Grifter" (Moore Creations) and "Lady Death" figures (Chaos Comics) were nicely done.

Lisa Snellings "dark carnival" pieces were evocative and fascinating while Theodore Gall achieved some amazing things with his surreal steel figures.

Tony McVey's Menagerie Productions released a ghoulish series of monster maquettes, including a nasty gargoyle and an equally chilling vampire. Miles Teves created a striking life-size bust of Boris Karloff as Frankenstein's monster for Cine Art and Sam Greenwell captured the "Rage of the Creature" in a kit for ResinHedz. Sideshow Productions released an extremely intricate model based on *Bernie Wrightson's Frankenstein* (sculpted by Dan Platt,) Terry Lattimer interpreted Oscar Chichoni's *Heavy Metal* cover, "The Embrace," into 3-D for Streamline, and Steve West's nude "Demoness" for Cellar Cast was...hotter than hell. (I *had* to say it. Spank me.)

Japanese sculptor Juyi Oniki produced the lovely "Gillutina" (based on a comic by Yasushi Nirasawa) for Fewture Models while Takayuki Takeya sculpted the similarly marvelous "Guin" and "Albinone" (inspired by Michael Moorcock's sword & sorcery character, Elric) for the Yoshitaka Amano Collection.

DC also was responsible for a shelf-full of fine works throughout the year, including a set of Sandman bookends (designed by Michael Zuli,) a Swamp Thing figure, and a massive tribute to Batman and Robin (designed by Frank Miller,) all sculpted by William Paquet.

If you could think of it, there was a model kit or sculpture of it out there somewhere. Dragons? Sure. Scream Queens? Plenty. Comics characters? More than you could wave a cape at. I even ran across a Mutley (*Mutley*?!) model from Saturday morning cartoons.

INSTITUTIONAL

▼

"Institutional" is a vast melting-pot category that includes trading cards, calendars, prints, gallery posters, promotional art, computer game graphics...you name it. There was an infinite variety of formats and venues for fantastic art. All you had to do was look.

The bloom was off the trading card business after several years of rapid growth. '95's slump continued through 1996 and there were fewer offerings on the market. FPG released sets by Don Maitz (his second), Thomas Canty, Janny Wurts, and Jeffrey Jones; Topps' *Star Wars Galaxy III* included nice art by Jack Davis, Gahan Wilson, and Therese Nielsen while their *Goosebumps 2* set featured John Pound and Zina Saunders; Wildstorm productions produced the saucy *Art of Joe Chiodo* set; Skybox's *Batman Master Series* showcased work by Dave Dorman, Dermot Powers, Duncan Fergredo and Carl Critchlow; and Dark Horse's *Madman X* consisted of other artists' interpretations of Mike Allred's hero, including art by Frank Frazetta, Brian Bolland, and Bill Tucci.

But it seemed that the most voracious arena for fantastic art was the role-playing game market—an industry whose phenomenal success was perhaps slightly tarnished by some negative media attention. One company's restructuring of artists' fees and card royalties caused grumbling in the press while some grisly murders by several devotees of another firm's vampire-themed games

Charles Burns was just one of the artists featured in Kitchen Sink Press' alternative holiday greetings.

had both tabloids and fundamentalists gleefully pointing fingers of blame.

None of which could diminish the wonderful work created for the gaming market. Wizards of the Coast's *Magic* (and attendant sets) featured work by, well, just about *everybody*, including Rob Bliss, Rick Berry, Donato Giancola,

Phil Hale, Rob Alexander, and Moebius, to name only a handful. FPG's *Dark Age* featured stunning work by Brom, John Berkey, John Bolton, Berry, Hale, and John Zeleznik while their *Guardian's* game was highlighted by the art of Keith Parkinson, Maitz, Brom, and Mike Ploog. White Wolf, Palladium, and FASA all featured worthy work by George Pratt, Jeff Laubenstein, Tim Bradstreet, and Jim Nelson among many others.

Scads of calendars were produced before the end of '96, including *100 Years of American Comics* (Walt Kelly, Al Capp, etc.,) *Morpheus International* (Ernst Fuchs, Clive Barker, etc.,) and DC's *Vertigo* (Charles Vess, Michael Zuli, etc.) Dave McKean, Michael Whelan, Luis Royo, Frank Frazetta, H.R. Giger, Boris, Jeff Smith, Carl Barks, and Gil Bruvel all had colorful calendars devoted to their work.

The Greenwich Workshop once again produced exceptional fine art prints by Thomas Blackshear II, Scott Gustafson, James Christensen, and Bev Doolittle; James Gurney was kept busy working on the *Dinotopia* film, prehistoric stamps for the post office, and other secret projects. He *did* find the time to provide the grand prize to the *Dinotopia* Poster Contest sponsored by Scholastic: students Kathryn Noel, Peter Im, Laura Blanco, Adrian Jeffers, Michael Almaraz, and Brian Harris were painted into a dinosaur parade to be published as a print in the summer of 1997 by Portal Publications.

Mill Pond Press released new work by Dean Morrissey, Graphitti Designs continued with their stunning line of James Bama's "Doc Savage" posters and prints, and Glass Onion produced a pair of hand-engraved, foil-etched lithographs by Michael Whelan, "Summer Queen" and "Snow Queen." Kitchen Sink Press closed the year with *Scenes From the Xenozoic Age* by Mark Schultz, perhaps the most lavish folio of frameable prints ever offered to the comics field, along

with a pair of 10-card multi-artist sets of "Seasoned Greetings" that were a refreshing alternative to the bland holiday offerings at the shopping mall.

James Cowen, owner of Morpheus International, opened Galerie Morpheus in Beverly Hills, CA. The gallery exhibited (and offered for sale) works by

Jim Cowen (posing with a De Es sculpture) opened Galerie Morpheus in California.

(among others) H.R. Giger, Ernst Fuchs, Wayne Barlowe, De Es, and Jacek Yerka.

The Canton Museum of Art (Canton, OH) sponsored the popular "Pavilions of Wonder," featuring many of the field's best artists. The Words & Pictures Museum (Northampton, MA,) The Cartoon Art Museum (San Francisco, CA,) Four Color Images (NYNY,) the Kemper Museum (KCMO,) and the International Museum of Cartoon Art (Boca Raton, FL) sponsored group and single artist exhibits that pleased virtually any taste.

Collector's of original art had many opportunities to purchase work from a variety of sources, including directly from some creators. Two of the most responsible by-mail dealers in original works included Jane Frank's Worlds of Wonder (P.O. Box 814, Mclean, VA 22101 [703] 790-9519) and Scott Dunbier/Wildstorm Fine Arts (P.O. Box 1981, La Jolla, CA 92038 [619] 551-9724).

HELP ME!

◆

If you produce work you think would be of interest or if you run across something worthy in your travels (particularly from overseas) drop me a card, send me a Xerox®, for goodness' sake *anything* to let me know! Sample products are always appreciated. Write to: Arnie Fenner/Spectrum, P.O. Box 4422, Overland Park, KS 66204-0422 USA.

THE CHESLEY AWARDS

The Chesley Awards are presented annually by the Association of Science Fiction & Fantasy Artists in recognition of works and achievements by individuals in a given year. For more information about the organization write to ASFA, P.O. Box 825, Lecanto, FL 34460.

Best Color Work/Unpublished:
Stephen Hickman for "The Archers of Lhune"

Best Cover Illustration/Magazine:
Bob Eggleton (*Analog SF* 1/95)

Best Three-Dimensional Art:
Barclay Shaw for "Wonderland"

Best Monochrome Work/Unpublished:
Todd Lockwood for "Cerebus"

Best Cover Illustration/Hardback:
Tom Kidd for *Kingdoms of the Night*

Best Interior Illustration:
James Gurney for *Dinotopia: The World Beneath*

Best Cover Illustration/Paperback:
Don Maitz for *A Farce to be Reckoned With*

Best Art Director: Jamie Warren Youll/Bantam Spectra
Award for Artistic Achievement: Thomas Canty
Award for Contribution to ASFA: Ingrid Neilson

The Show

artist: **RICK BERRY**
art director: Carl Gnam   *client:* Science Fiction Age   *title:* Wintermute   *medium:* Red chalk/digital

artist: **BRAD HOLLAND**
art director: Tom Staebler   *designer:* Kerig Pope   *client:* Playboy Magazine   *title:* Physical 8/96

1
artist: **STU SUCHIT**
art director: Stephani Finns/Lisa Orsini
client: Mac User
title: Postscript Level 3
medium: Digital
size: 6 1/2"x6"

2
artist: **KERRY P. TALBOTT**
client: Richmond Times Dispatch
title: Stress: Tax Time
medium: Colored Pencil
size: 10"x16"

3
artist: **FRED FIELDS**
art director: Robin Ramos
client: Inquest Magazine
title: Come to Mummy
medium: Oil
size: 11"x16"

4
artist: **JOSEPH DeVITO**
art director: Jonathan Schneider
designer: Jonathan Schneider
client: Mad Magazine
medium: Oil
size: 18"x25"

2

3

4

4

1
artist: **WILSON McLEAN**
art director: Tom Staebler
designer: Tom Staebler
client: Playboy Magazine
title: The Ten Best
medium: Oil on canvas
size: 18"x18"

2
artist: **OMAR RAYYAN**
art director: Ron McCutchan
designer: Omar Rayyan
client: Spider Magazine
medium: Watercolor
size: 8"x10"

3
artist: **WOJTEK SIUDMAK**
art director: Terri Czeczko
client: Asimov's Science Fiction
medium: Mixed
size: 18"x24"

4
artist: **DAVID DORMAN**
art director: Dave Elliott
client: Penthouse Comix
title: Wasteland: End of the Line
medium: Oil
size: 14"x20"

1

3

2

1
artist: **RAY-MEL CORNELIUS**
client: Rough Magazine
title: Planet Punchatz
medium: Acrylic
size: 10¼"x10"

2
artist: **PATRICK ARRASMITH**
art director: Jeff Capaldi
designer: Jeff Capaldi
client: American Medical News
title: To Sleep, Perchance to Cure
medium: Scratchboard & acrylic
size: 11"x14"

3
artist: **GEORGE H. KRAUTER**
art director: Terri Czeczko
designer: George H. Krauter
client: Analog
title: Primrose
medium: Digital

4
artist: **BRAD WEINMAN**
art director: Nancy Duckworth
designer: Nancy Duckworth
client: Los Angeles Times Magazine
title: Starbuck's Alien
medium: Oil
size: 9"x12"

1
artist: **ISTVAN BANYAI**
art director: Tom Staebler
designer: Kerig Pope
client: Playboy Magazine
title: In the Upper Room

2
artist: **GUY BILLOUT**
art director: Tom Staebler
designer: Len Willis
client: Playboy Magazines
title: Black Water, Deep Canyon

3
artist: **ILENE MEYER**
client: Fuji Television Network/Japan
title: Medusa
medium: Oil
size: 23"x30"

artist: **RAFAL OLBINSKI**

designer: Rafal Olbinski   *client:* The New York City Opera   *title:* Falstaff   *medium:* Acrylic

artist: **STEPHAN "CRICKET" MARTINIERE**
art director: Julian Corbett   *client:* Media Lab   *title:* Eden   *medium:* Digital

1
artist: **DiTERLIZZI**
art director: Rich Tomas
designer: Larry Snelly
client: White Wolf Games
title: Sidhe Noble
medium: Watercolor
size: 20"x30"

2
artist: **NICHOLAS GAETANO**
art director: Nina Scerbo
client: Seasons
title: Anxiety
medium: Acrylic
size: 4 1/2"x15"

3
artist: **RAFAL OLBINSKI**
designer: Rafal Olbinski
client: The New York City Opera
medium: Acrylic

GOTTFRIED VON EINEM
THE VISIT of the OLD LADY
OPERA IN 3 ACTS AFTER FRIEDRICH DÜRRENMAT'S TRAGI-COMEDY

NEW · YORK · CITY · OPERA

1
artist: **JILL BAUMAN**
designer: Jill Bauman
client: Doubleday Direct
title: Dark Assortment
medium: Acrylic
size: 16"x18"

2
artist: **JOHN RUSH**
art director: Ken Brockaway
client: Zurich-American Insurance Co.
title: Gulliver Arrives in Lilliput
medium: Oil
size: 40"x14"

3
artist: **RAFAL OLBINSKI**
designer: Rafal Olbinski
client: The New York City Opera
medium: Acrylic

1
artist: **WES BENSCOTER**
designer: Wes Benscoter
client: Metal Blade Records
title: Loathing
medium: Acrylic
size: 18"x18"

2
artist: **MARK SASSO**
art director: Ed Goldberg & Dat Lahm
client: Mattel Toys
title: T-Bone
medium: Acrylic
size: 12"x12"

3
artist: **WILLIAM STOUT**
art director: William Stout
designer: William Stout
client: Monstrosities, Inc.
medium: Inks, colored pencils, watercolor on board

1

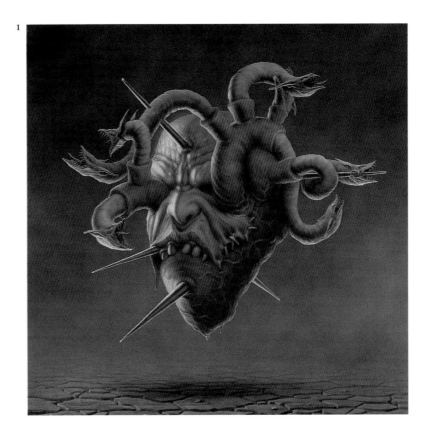

2

3

artist: **JOHN JUDE PALENCAR**
art director: Betsy Wollheim & Sheila Gilbert   *client:* Daw Books   *title:* Blood Debt   *medium:* Acrylic   *size:* 21"x27"

artist: **JAMES C. CHRISTENSEN**
art director: Scott Usher   *designer:* Peter Landa   *client:* The Greenwich Workshop & Artisan Press
title: Court of the Fairies   *medium:* Oil   *size:* 60"x40"

1
artist: **ROBH RUPPEL**
art director: Bruce Zamjahn
client: TSR Books
title: F.R.E.E. Fall
medium: Oil
size: 20"x30"

2
artist: **PAUL ALEXANDER**
art director: Jim Baen
client: Baen Books
title: The Bavarian Gate
medium: Gouache
size: 14"x23"

3
artist: **JOHN HARRIS**
art director: Irene Gallo
client: Tor Books
title: A Million Open Doors II
medium: Acrylic
size: 16"x24"

4
artist: **GNEMO**
art director: Tom Kidd
designer: Michael Brocha
client: Norwescon
title: Port Rockwell
medium: Oil
size: 24"x36"

1
artist: **SERGEI GOLOSHAPOV**
art director: Sergei Goloshapov
client: North-South Books
title: The Six Servants
medium: Watercolor
size: 16"x23 1/8"

2
artist: **MICHAEL WHELAN**
art director: Arnie Fenner
designer: Arnie Fenner
client: Mark V. Ziesing Books
title: Something In My Eye
medium: Oil on board
size: 22"x22"

3
artist: **ROBERT CRUMB**
art director: Amie Brockway
designer: Lisa Stone
client: Kitchen Sink Press
title: Kafka
medium: Ink
size: 8 1/2"x11"

4
artist: **JOHN K. SNYDER III**
art director: Harlan Ellison &
           Larry S. Friedman
client: White Wolf Books
title: Harlan Ellison's Edgeworks #2

1

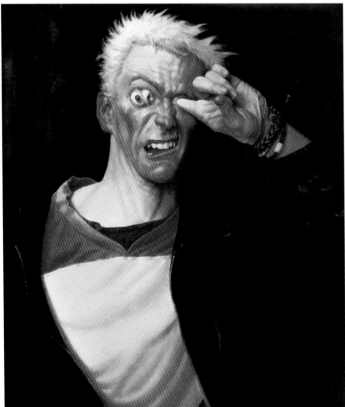

2

3

1
artist: **VICTOR LEE**
art director: Lisa Peters
designer: Lisa Peters
client: Harcourt Brace & Co.
title: Little Sister
medium: Acrylic
size: 10"x15"

2
artist: **DOUG BEEKMAN**
art director: Peter Lutjen
client: Tor Books
title: Conan & the Grim Grey God
medium: Mixed
size: 38"x27"

3
artist: **DON MAITZ**
art director: Carl Galian
client: Roc Books
title: Merlin's Harp
medium: Oil
size: 20"x30"

1
artist: **CHRIS MOORE**
art director: Madeline Mechiffe
client: Harper Collins
title: We Can Build You
medium: Acrylic
size: 22½"x17"

2
artist: **FRANK KELLY FREAS**
art director: Jennifer Greenwell
client: The Easton Press
title: Brothers
medium: Acrylic
size: 16"x20"

3
artist: **RON WALOTSKY**
art director: Carl Galian
client: Penguin/Roc
title: Ancient Echoes
medium: Acrylic
size: 20"x30"

4
artist: **PAUL R. ALEXANDER**
art director: Jim Baen
client: Baen Books
title: Bolos 4: Last Stand
medium: Gouache
size: 14"x23"

1

2

3

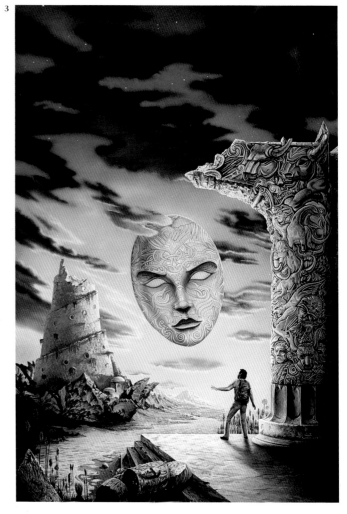

1
artist: **SERGEI GOLOSHAPOV**
art director: Sergei Goloshapov
client: North-South Books
title: The Six Servants
medium: Watercolor
size: 16"x13 1/8"

2
artist: **JAMES C. CHRISTENSEN**
art director: Scott Usher
designer: Peter Landa
client: The Greenwich Workshop/
　　　　　Artisan Press
title: Sisters of the Sea
medium: Oil
size: 40"x30"

3
artist: **JEFF LAUBENSTEIN**
art director: Jim Nelson
client: FASA Corporation
title: Serpent Riverview
medium: Oil
size: 24"x36"

1

LAUBENSTEIN '96

1
artist: **GARY A. LIPPINCOTT**
art director: Michael Farmer
designer: Lisa Peters
client: Harcourt Brace & Co.
title: Tomorrow's Wizard
medium: Watercolor
size: 10"x16"

2
artist: **GARY RUDDELL**
art director: Jim Baen
client: Baen Books
title: Lost Children
medium: Oil
size: 16"x23"

3
artist: **DONATO GIANCOLA**
art director: David Stevenson
client: Ballantine Books
title: Mother of Winter
medium: Oil on paper
size: 34"x22"

4
artist: **ROMAS KUKALIS**
art director: Sheila Gilbert
client: Daw Books
title: Ghost Shadows
medium: Acrylic on board
size: 19"x28"

1

2

3

1
artist: **JAMES WARHOLA**
art director: Jim Frenkel
designer: Carol Russo
client: Tor Books
title: Callahan's Legacy
medium: Oil
size: 25"x25"

2
artist: **JOHN JUDE PALENCAR**
art director: David Stevenson
designer: John Jude Palencar
client: Random House/Ballantine Books
title: The Transition of H.P. Lovecraft:
        The Road to Madness
medium: Acrylic
size: 19"x15"

3
artist: **CAROL HEYER**
art director: Tama Montgomery
designer: Ideals C.B. Staff
client: Ideals Children's Books
title: Dragonwing Faerie: Sleeping Beauty
medium: Acrylic
size: 18"x24"

4
artist: **DON MAITZ**
art director: Robert Wiener
designer: Tom Canty
client: Donald M. Grant Books
title: Desperation: The Cop
medium: Oil
size: 11"x14"

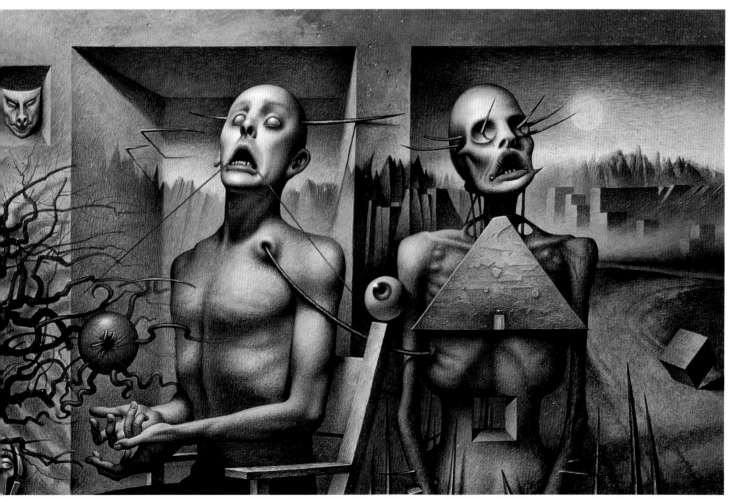

2

1
artist: **LAUREN MILLS**
art director: Amelia Carling
client: Dial Books
title: The Book of Little Folk
medium: Watercolor
size: 10"x12 1/2"

2
artist: **GLENN KIM**
art director: Judy Murello
designer: Judy Murello
client: Berkley Books
title: Dragon Burning
medium: Acrylic
size: 6"x20"

3
artist: **DENNIS NOLAN**
art director: Atha Tehon
client: Dial Books
title: A Midsummer Night's Dream
medium: Watercolor
size: 14"x16"

1

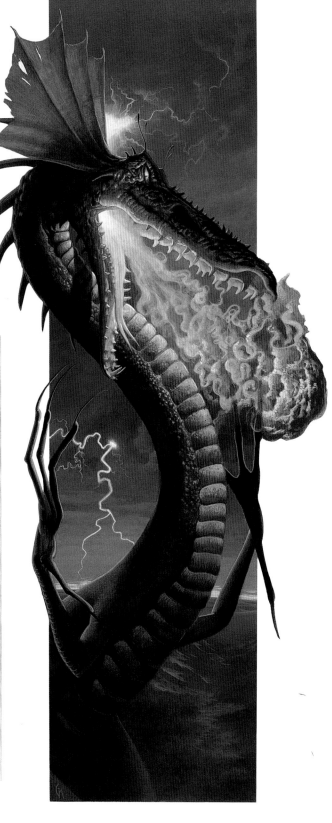

1
artist: **BRUCE JENSEN**
art director: David Stevenson
designer: David Stevenson
client: Ballantine Books
title: Do Androids Dream of Electric Sheep?
medium: Acrylic
size: 16"x22"

2
artist: **CHRIS MOORE**
art director: Madeline Mechiffe
client: Harper Collins
title: Do Androids Dream of Electric Sheep?
medium: Acrylic
size: 21"x16"

3
artist: **DONATO GIANCOLA**
client: Warner Books
title: Ravengers
medium: Oil on paper
size: 18"x32"

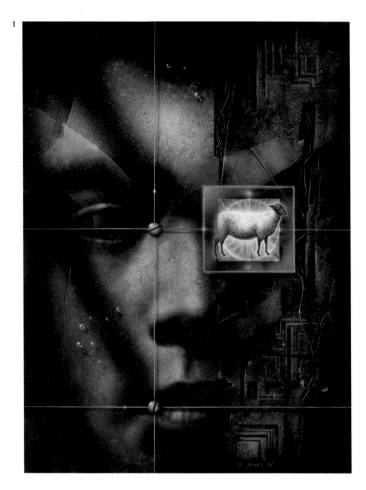

3

1
artist: **JOHN JUDE PALENCAR**
art director: Don Puckey
designer: Don Puckey
client: Warner Books
title: Imago
medium: Acrylic
size: 14"x14"

2
artist: **DONATO GIANCOLA**
client: Penguin/Roc
title: The Dragonstone
medium: Oil on paper
size: 34"x22"

3
artist: **STEPHEN YOULL**
art director: Jamie S. Warren
designer: Stephen Youll
client: Bantam Books
title: Exile's Challenge
medium: Oil
size: 33½"x23½"

1

2

1
artist: **JAMES NELSON**
art director: James Nelson
client: FASA Corporation
title: Ktenshin Tower
medium: Watercolor
size: 9 3/4"x13 3/4"

2
artist: **STEPHEN HICKMAN**
art director: Jim Baen
designer: Stephen Hickman
client: Baen Books
title: The Card Master
medium: Oil
size: 19"x30"

3
artist: **GNEMO**
art director: Tom Kidd
designer: Michael Brocha
client: Norwescon
medium: Oil

4
artist: **PAUL YOULL**
art director: Jamie S. Warren Youll
designer: Paul Youll
client: Bantam Books/LucasFilm Ltd.
title: Star Wars X Wing: The Bacta War
medium: Oil/acrylic
size: 19"x27"

1

2

3

4

1
artist: **STEPHEN YOULL**
art director: Don Puckey
designer: Stephen Youll
client: Warner Books
title: Finity's End
medium: Oil
size: 16"x21 1/2"

2
artist: **JIM BURNS**
art director: Gene Mydlowski
designer: Rich Hasselberger
client: Harper/Prism
title: Sorcerers of Majipoor
medium: Acrylic
size: 30"x18"

3
artist: **STEPHEN HICKMAN**
art director: James Baen
designer: Stephen Hickman
client: Baen Books
title: Drakon
medium: Oil
size: 16"x26"

1
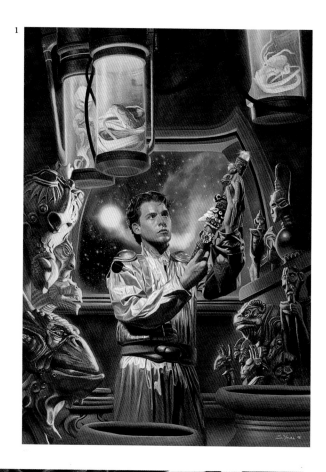

2

1
artist: **JOHN JUDE PALENCAR**
art director: Don Puckey
designer: Don Puckey
client: Warner Books
title: Adulthood Rites
medium: Acrylic
size: 14"x14"

2
artist: **BRYN BARNARD**
art director: Susan White
client: Time-Life Books
title: Eden
medium: Acrylic
size: 24"x14"

3
artist: **VICTOR LEE**
art director: Victor Lee
designer: Aileen Friedman
client: Bridgewater Books
title: Flight of the Dragons
medium: Acrylic
size: 18"x12"

4
artist: **JAMES C. CHRISTENSEN**
art director: Scott Usher
designer: Peter Landa
client: The Greenwich Workshop/
      Artisan Press
title: The Royal Processional
medium: Oil
size: 48"x24"

1

2

1
artist: **DOUGLAS SMITH**
art director: Joseph Montebello
designer: Joel Avirom
client: Regan Books/Harper Collins
title: Wicked
medium: Scratchboard & watercolor
size: 9½"x14½"

2
artist: **NICHOLAS JAINSCHIGG**
art director: Irene Gallo
client: Tor Books
title: Wildside [paperback]
medium: Mixed/assemblage
size: 18"x24"

3
artist: **DOUGLAS SMITH**
art director: Joseph Montebello
designer: Joel Avirom
client: Regan Books/Harper Collins
title: The Murder and It's Afterlife
medium: Scratchboard
size: 6"x9½"

4
artist: **TRISTAN A. ELWELL**
art director: Irene Gallo
client: Tor Books
title: The Willing Spirit
medium: Acrylic on masonite
size: 18"x24"

1
artist: **GNEMO**
art director: Tom Kidd
designer: Michael Brocha
client: Norwescon
title: Peale's New York Penthouse
medium: Oil
size: 30"x40"

2
artist: **DANIEL BRERETON**
art director: Larry Snelly
designer: Daniel Brereton
client: White Wolf
title: Midnight Circus
medium: Watercolor
size: 12"x19"

3
artist: **BOLTON BOROS & CABOR SZIKSZAI**
designer: Bolton Boros & Cabor Seikszai
client: Mora SF [Budapest]
title: The World of Baphomet
medium: Acrylic
size: 8"x13"

4
artist: **JOHN HOWE**
art director: Sheila Gilbert
designer: Miles Long
client: Daw Books
title: The Cloak of Night and Daggers
medium: Watercolor
size: 18"x30"

1

2

3

1
artist: **BOB EGGLETON**
art director: Irene Gallo
client: Tor Books
title: Saturn Ruhk
medium: Acrylic
size: 30"x20"

2
artist: **ALAN POLLACK**
art director: Bob Galica
designer: Dawn Murin
client: TSR Books
title: Planar Powers
medium: Oil
size: 23"x38"

3
artist: **LUIS ROYO**
art director: Luis Royo
client: Norma Editorial
title: Window Towards Buonarroti
medium: Acrylic & ink
size: 14"x24"

4
artist: **KEITH PARKINSON**
art director: Kevin Siembieda
designer: Keith Parkinson
client: Palladium Books, Inc.
title: Eandroth Rider
medium: Oil
size: 24"x30"

1

2

3

artist: **DOUG BEEKMAN**

art director: Denny O'Neil & Mark Chiarello   *client:* DC Comics   *title:* Shadow of the Bat   *medium:* Watercolor   *size:* 16"x26"

artist: **MARK SCHULTZ**

art director: Amie Brockway   designer: Kevin Lison   client: Kitchen Sink Press   title: Xenozoic Tales #14
medium: Ink & digital color   size: 14"x20"

1
artist: **RAY LAGO**
art director: Mark Mazz
client: Harris Comics
title: Vampirella's 25th Anniversary
medium: Watercolor
size: 12"x19"

2
artist: **MARK NELSON**
art director: Amie Brockway
designer: Douglas Bantz
client: Kitchen Sink Press
title: Death Rattle
medium: Ink & digital color
size: 11"x17"

3
artist: **PAOLO PARENTE**
art director: Dan Raspler
designer: Paolo Parente
client: DC Comics
title: Good Boy!
medium: Acrylic

4
artist: **RAY LAGO**
art director: Mark Mazz
client: Harris Comics
title: Vampirella's 25th Anniversary
medium: Watercolor
size: 12"x19"

4

57

1
artist: **MARK WHEATLEY**
art director: Mark Wheatley
client: Mark's Giant Economy
        Size Comics
title: Radical Dreamer Prime
medium: Dyes, gouache, digital
size: 13¼"x10¼"

2
artist: **STEVE RUDE**
client: Dark Horse Comics
title: Alien Justice
medium: Colored inks
size: 20"x30"

3
artist: **JIM LEE**
art director: Mike Heisler
designer: Greg Brotherton
client: Wildstorm Productions
title: Deathblow #0
medium: Pencil & ink
size: 11"x17"

4
artist: **STEVE RUDE**
client: Dark Horse Comics
title: Sunny Day
medium: Acrylic
size: 20"x30"

1
artist: **DAVE McKEAN**
art director: Amie Brockway
designer: Dave McKean
client: Kitchen Sink Press
title: Cages #10
medium: Mixed/digital

2
artist: **REBECCA GUAY**
art director: Jeff Gomez
client: Acclaim Comics
title: Feroz and Serra
medium: Watercolor
size: 11"x14"

3
artist: **STEVE RUDE**
client: Dark Horse Comics
title: The Dark Side of the Moon
medium: Oil
size: 20"x30"

4
artist: **ALEX ROSS**
client: Wildstorm Productions
title: Astro City

1
artist: **JOHN MUELLER**
art director: Amie Brockway
designer: Evan Metcalf
client: Kitchen Sink Press
title: The Crow: Wild Justice
medium: Mixed/acrylic
size: 15"x21"

2
artist: **CHARLES BURNS**
art director: Amie Brockway
client: Kitchen Sink Press
title: Black Hole #3
medium: Ink
size: 14"x20"

3
artist: **JACQUES BREDY**
art director: Mike Lund
designer: Cebal
client: Vert-H
medium: Oil
size: 14"x17"

4
artist: **STEVE FASTNER & RICH LARSON**
art director: Sal Quartuccio
designer: Rich Larson
client: SQ Productions, Inc.
title: Demon Baby vs Bane
medium: Airbrush & markers
size: 11"x17"

1
artist: **MARK GABBANA**
client: Rudy Coby
title: Labman
medium: Acrylic
size: 10 1/2"x16"

2
artist: **CLYDE CALDWELL**
client: Armada Comics
title: Fallen Angel
medium: Oil
size: 12 5/8"x18 7/8"

3
artist: **GREG LOUDON**
art director: Hart Fisher
client: Boneyard Press
title: Vampire Lust #1
medium: Acrylic
size: 18"x24"

4
artist: **DAVID DeVRIES**
art director: Bob Kahan
client: DC Comics
title: Batman/Superman
medium: Acrylic

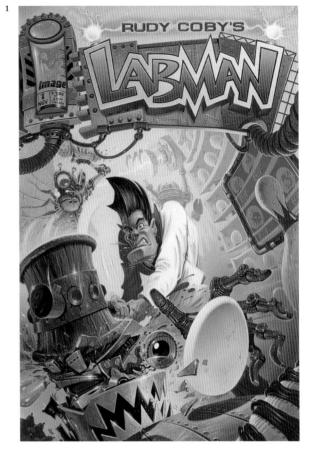

4

©DAVE DeVries '96

1
artist: **TRAVIS CHAREST**
art director: Mike Heisler
client: Wildstorm Productions
title: WildC.A.T.S. #28
medium: Ink
size: 11"x17"

2
artist: **GLEN ORBICK**
art director: Dan Raspler
client: DC Comics
title: The Spectre #49
medium: Oil
size: 16"x22"

3
artist: **JOHN MUELLER**
art director: Amie Brockway
designer: Evan Metcalf
client: Kitchen Sink Press
title: The Crow: Wild Justice
medium: Mixed
size: 18"x24"

artist: **JOSEPH DeVITO**

designer: Burne Hogarth   *client:* Graphitti Design   *title:* The Hogarth Tarzan   *medium:* Bronze   *size:* 15"H

artist: **J.A. PIPPETT**
art director: J.A. Pippett   *designer:* J.A. Pippett   *title:* MoonLighter   *medium:* Patina/bronze   *size:* 31"H

1
artist: **RANDY BOWEN**
art director: Sue Ann Harkey
client: Magic: The Gathering
title: Shivan Dragon

2
artist: **HARRIETT MORTEN-BECKER**
designer: Harriett Morten Becker
client: Nocturnal Vision
title: Starlight
medium: Clay
size: 10"H

3
artist: **CLAYBURN S. MOORE**
art director: Clayburn S. Moore
designer: Clayburn S. Moore
client: Frank Frazetta
title: Princess
medium: Bronze
size: 10 1/2"H

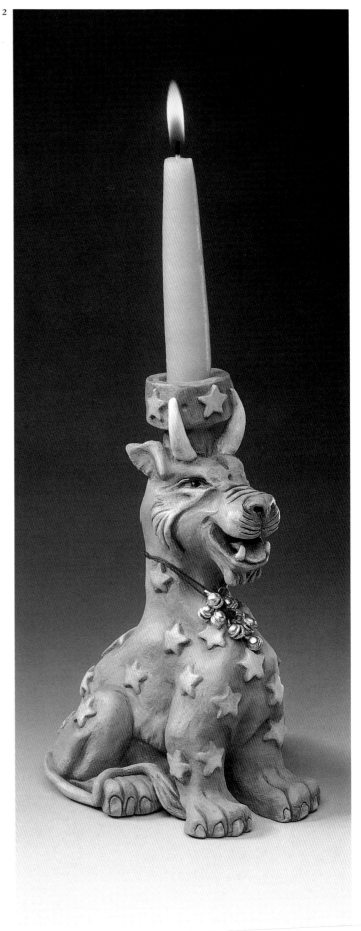

1
artist: **MAT FALLS**
client: Sideshow, Inc.
title: Alien Grey
medium: Clay & resin
size: 10"Hx10"Dx9"W

2
artist: **ANTHONY VEILLEUX**
designer: Anthony Veilleux
client: G-Force Model Kits Canada
title: Guller's Daughter
medium: Mixed/resin

3
artist: **CLAYBURN S. MOORE**
art director: Clayburn S. Moore
designer: Clayburn S. Moore
client: Top Cow Productions
title: Witchblade
medium: Cold-cast porcelain
size: 11 1/2"H

4
artist: **SAM GREENWELL**
designer: Sam Greenwell
client: Acornboy Studios/Nemesis
title: Aries
medium: Super Sculpey
size: 16"H

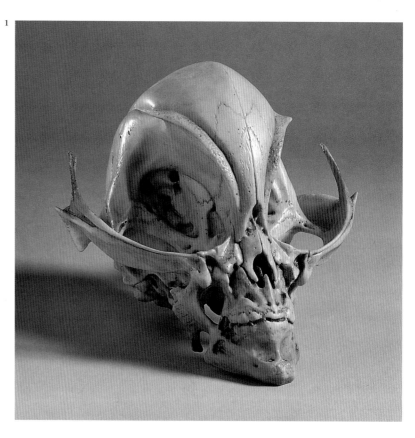

1
artist: **MILES TEVES**
art director: Miles Teves
designer: Gino Acevedo
client: CinéArt
title: The Monster
medium: Polyresin
size: 16"x20"

2
artist: **LISA SNELLINGS**
designer: Lisa Snelling
client: L.S. Dark Caravan
title: A Measure of Grace
medium: Wood/clay
size: 12"H

3
artist: **TOM TAGGART**
art director: Dan Raspler
photographer: Sal Trombino
client: DC Comics
title: Spectre Spider
medium: Super Sculpey

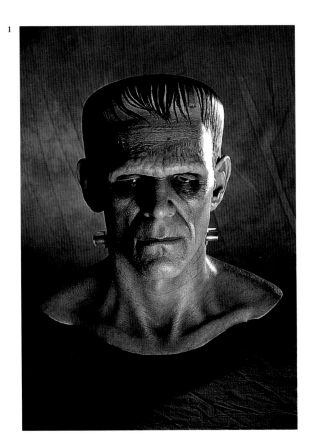

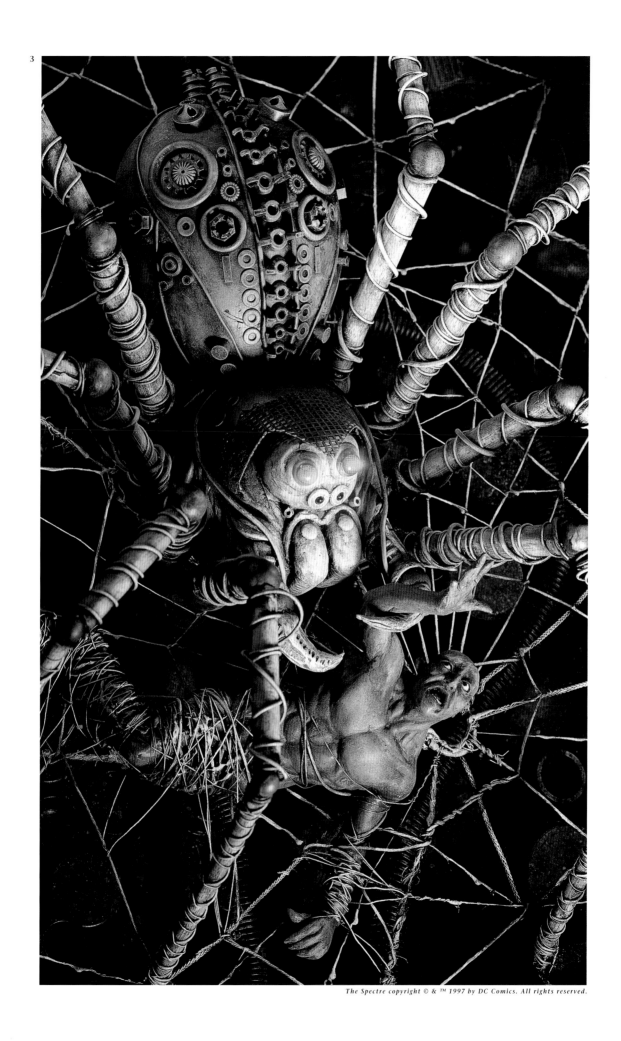

1
artist: **OLIVER McCRAE**
client: Eagle Heart Createlier
title: Homage to Roger Stine
medium: Ceramic
size: 12"Hx10"Wx9"D

2
artist: **OLIVER McCRAE**
client: Eagle Heart Createlier
title: Behold Unto Us a Manchild is Born
        and His Name Shall Be Wonderful,
        and Mighty God
medium: Ceramic
size: 24"Hx15"Wx16"D

3
artist: **JOEL HARLOW**
art director: Joel Harlow
title: Great Old One
medium: Bronze
size: 1'x2'

artist: **PHIL HALE**
art director: Brom   *client:* FPG   *medium:* Oil   *size:* 13"x16"

artist: **PETAR MESELDŽIJA**
art director: Chris Meiklejohn   *designer:* Petar Meseldžija   *client:* Meiklejohn Graphics   *title:* Noble Dragon
medium: Oil   *size:* 50cmx70cm

1
artist: **YURI BARTOLI**
designer: Yuri Bartoli
client: Yuri Bartoli
title: Whale's Sky
medium: Oil
size: 20"x15"

2
artist: **PHILIP STRAUB**
art director: Philip Straub
title: Faceplate
medium: Oil
size: 11"x14"

3
artist: **GREG & TIM HILDEBRANDT**
art director: Ingar Westburg
client: Topps Company
title: Vader Destroys the Rebel Base
medium: Acrylic
size: 11"x15"

4
artist: **MIKE EVANS**
designer: Mike Evans
client: The School of Visual Arts
title: Number 16
medium: Oil
size: 13"x20"

1

2

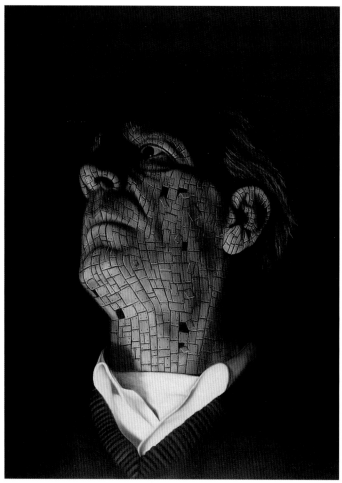

3

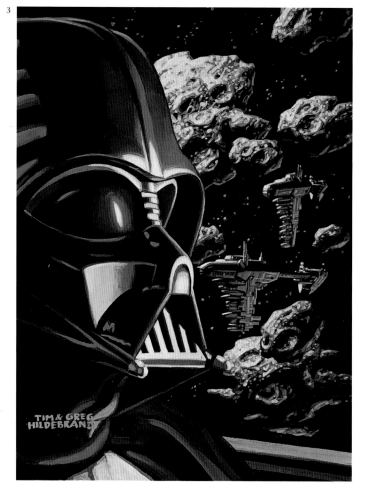

1
artist: **FRED HOOPER**
art director: C.J. Carrella
designer: Gary Sibley
client: Myrmidon Press
title: Abomination Codox
medium: Digital
size: 8"x10"

2
artist: **MURRAY TINKELMAN**
art director: Joe Glisson
designer: Joe Glisson
client: Dellas Graphics
title: Horror Frog
medium: Color inks
size: 11"x18"

3
artist: **DARREL ANDERSON**
art director: Darrel Anderson
client: Braid Media Arts
title: Thorn Temple 1
medium: Digital

4
artist: **RICK BERRY**
art director: Brom/Rick Berry
designer: Brom
client: FPG
title: Khimera
medium: Oil/digital

1
artist: **GREG NEWBOLD**
art director: Steve Owen
designer: Chris Johnson
client: Brodart Co.
title: Looking For a Good Book
medium: Acrylic
size: 12"x12"

2
artist: **SEAN BEAVERS**
art director: Sean Beavers
client: Thanks To Gravity Inc.
title: Rain On the Hill
medium: Oil
size: 20"x22"

3
artist: **JAEL**
art director: Moira Clinch
designer: Graham Davis
client: Running Press
title: The Dream Lives
medium: Oil
size: 26"x32"

4
artist: **ERIC BOWMAN**
art director: Eric Bowman
title: Back To the Future
medium: Acrylic/prismacolor
size: 11 3/4"x15 3/8"

1
artist: **DAVID W. MEIKLE**
art director: Scott Greer
designer: Lisa Brashear
client: University of Utah
title: Medusa
medium: Acrylic
size: 9"x9"

2
artist: **WES BENSCOTER**
designer: Wes Benscoter
client: Midnight Mass
title: Rain On the Hill
medium: Acrylic
size: 24"x18"

3
artist: **RICHARD BOBER**
art director: Mat Tepper
client: Tamar Fantasy Prints
title: Dragon Fall
medium: Acrylic/oil
size: 30"x40"

1

2

1
artist: **WILLIAM PROSSER**
title: When Pigs Fly
medium: Oil
size: 44"x36"

2
artist: **DiTERLIZZI**
art director: Angela DeFrancis
client: Self-published print
title: Titania's Procession
medium: Airbrush/watercolor
size: 40"x30"

3
artist: **SCOTT GUSTAFSON**
art director: Jennifer Oakes
designer: Scott Gustafson
client: The Greenwich Workshop
title: Puss In Boots
medium: Oil
size: 30"x36"

1

2

3

1
artist: **JOEL BISKE**
client: Wizards of the Coast
title: Raven
medium: Acrylic
size: 10"x8"

2
artist: **BROM**
art director: Brom
designer: Brom
client: FPG
title: Peace
medium: Oil
size: 8"x10"

3
artist: **RICK BERRY**
art director: Brom
designer: Brom
client: FPG
title: Headball Tourney
medium: Watercolor/digital

4
artist: **JOE CHIODO**
art director: Ted Adams
designer: John Uhrich
client: Wildstorm Productions
title: Ladytron Internet
medium: Acrylic
size: 9"x12"

1

2

3

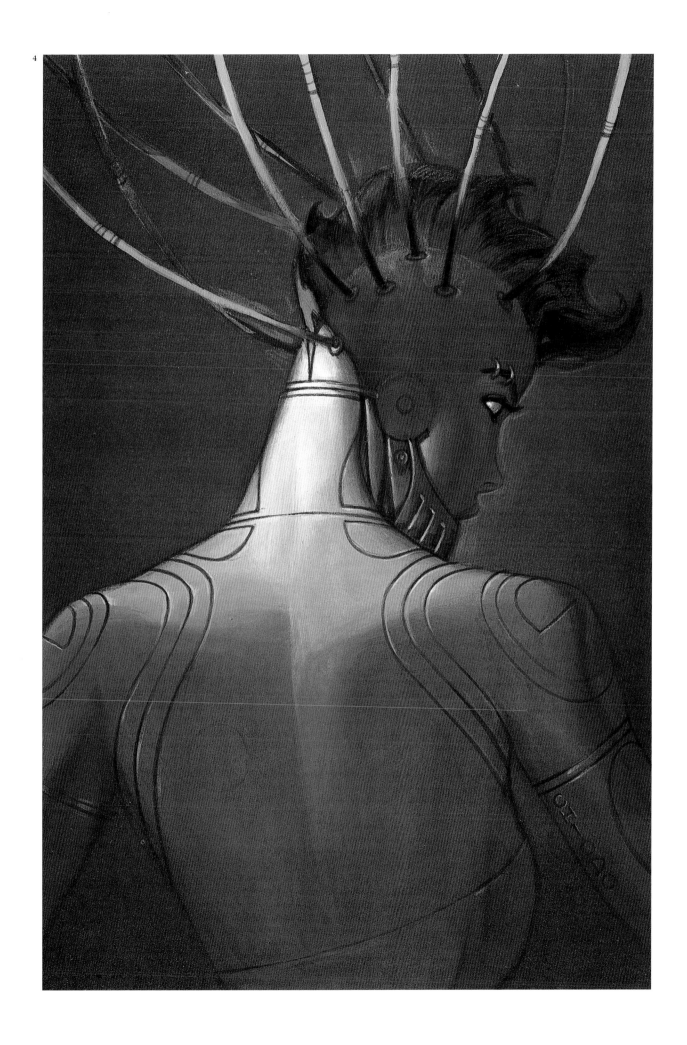

1
artist: **JAMES A. OWEN**
client: Dynamic Forces
title: Homer: Starchild Trading Cards
medium: Ink/marker/color pencil
size: 5"x7"

2
artist: **JAMES GURNEY**
art director: Collette Carter
client: Portal Publications
title: Kids and Dinosaurs
medium: Oil
size: 57"x19"

3
artist: **JEFF MIRACOLA**
art director: Stefan Ljungquist
designer: Jeff Miracola
client: Target Games
title: Lutherian Horseman
medium: Oil on board
size: 15"x17"

4
artist: **JOSEPH PAGE KOVACH**
art director: Joseph Page Kovach
designer: Joseph Page Kovach
client: American Showcase
title: Waste Land
medium: Mixed
size: 12"x19"

1

2

3

4

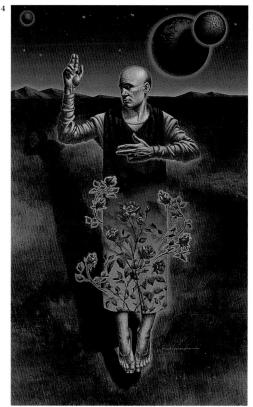

1
artist: **DAVID BOWERS**
title: O.J.'s Nightmare
medium: Oil
size: 12 1/2"x16 3/4"

2
artist: **TODD SCHORR**
art director: Amie K. Brockway
designer: Kevin Lison
client: Kitchen Sink Press
title: H.P. Lovecraft's Fried Seafood Cart
medium: Acrylic
size: 40"x30"

3
artist: **DAVID BOWERS**
art director: Frank Sturges
title: The Bird Keeper
medium: Oil
12 1/2"x17"

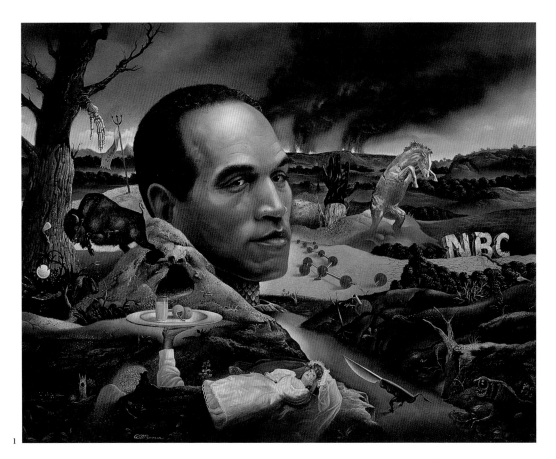

1
artist: **PHIL HALE**
art director: Craig Hooper
client: Wizards of the Coast
title: Fix All
medium: Oil

2
artist: **MOEBIUS**
art director: Craig Hooper
client: Wizards of the Coast
title: Project Zurich

3
artist: **BROM**
art director: Brom
designer: Brom
client: FPG
title: Grafter
medium: Oil
size: 8"x10"

1
artist: **MARK FISHMAN**
title: Bring On Halloween
medium: Oil
size: 18″x24″

2
artist: **GREG & TIM HILDEBRANDT**
art director: Dan Buckley
client: Fleer/Skybox
title: Bloody Mary
medium: Acrylic
size: 16″x21″

3
artist: **ZOLTON BOROS**
   & GABOR SZIKSZAI
designer: Zolton Boros
   & Gabor Szikszai
client: Hungaria Insurance Co.
title: Calendar—July/August
medium: Acrylic
size: 16″x10″

4
artist: **JOHN ZELEZNIK**
designer: John Zeleznik
client: Palladium Books
title: Rifts: Psyscape
medium: Acrylic
size: 18″x24″

1
artist: **GEOFF DARROW**
art director: Sue Ann Harkey
designer: Visions
client: Magic: The Gathering
title: Goblin Swine

2
artist: **ROBERT BLISS**
art director: Sue Ann Harkey
designer: "Mirage"
client: Magic: The Gathering
title: Polymorph

3
artist: **JOE WILSON**
art director: Joe Wilson
client: Self promotion
title: You Can't Make An Omelet...
medium: Oil
size: 13"x20 1/2"

1

2

1
artist: **TODD SCHORR**
art director: Amie K. Brockway
designer: Kevin Lison
client: Kitchen Sink Press
title: The Planet of Lost
medium: Acrylic
size: 40"x30"

2
artist: **JOE CHIODO**
art director: Ted Adams
designer: John Uhrich
client: Wildstorm Productions
title: Artemis, Fried Lizard
medium: Acrylic
size: 9"x12"

3
artist: **DAVID DeVRIES**
art director: Mike Pasciullo
client: Fleer/Skybox
title: Carnage
medium: Acrylic

4
artist: **FRED FIELDS**
client: S.Q. Productions
title: Immortality
medium: Oil
size: 11¼"x14¼"

1

2

3

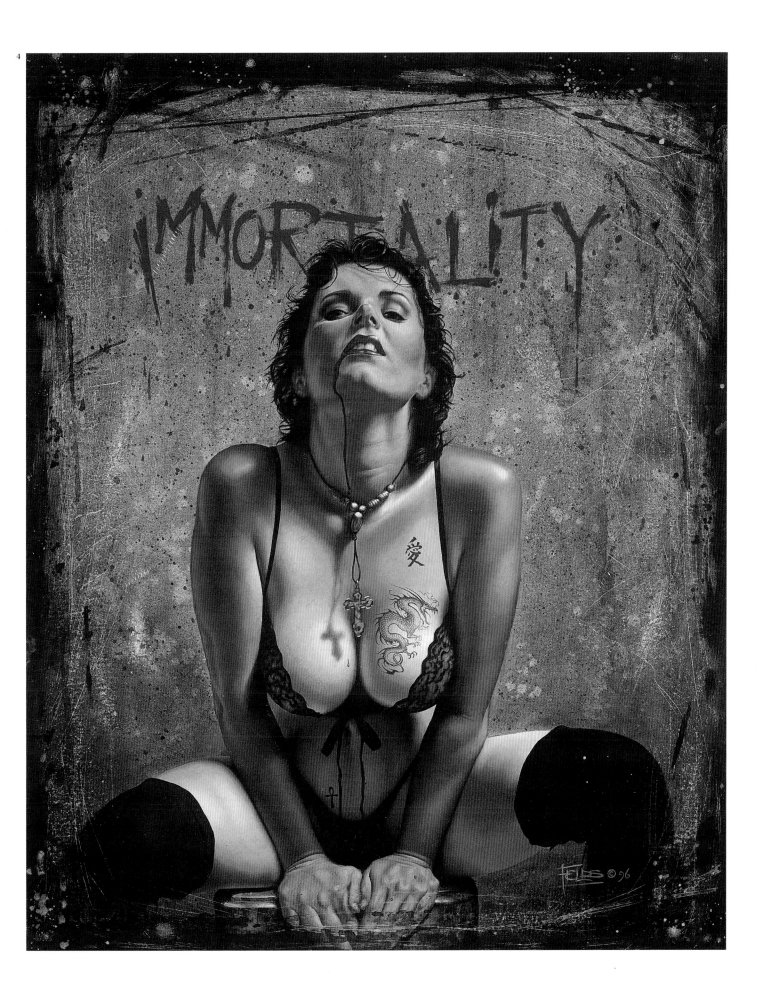

1
artist: **TERESE NIELSEN**
art director: Sue Ann Harkey
designer: Sue Ann Harkey
client: Wizards of the Coast
title: Foresight
medium: Mixed
size: 10"x8½"

2
artist: **RICK BERRY**
art director: Brom & Rick Berry
designer: Brom
client: FPG
title: CyberCop
medium: Watercolor/digital

3
artist: **PHIL HALE**
art director: Phil Hale
medium: Oil

4
artist: **RICK BERRY**
art director: Brom/Rick Berry
designer: Brom
client: FPG
title: Warchest
medium: Metal/watercolor/digital

1

2

3

1
artist: **RICK BERRY**
art director: Craig Hooper
client: Wizards of the Coast
title: Cybertech Think Tank
medium: Digital

2
artist: **SEAN COONS**
art director: Sean Coons
client: Plan-B
title: Grinch's Grinch
medium: Gouache
size: 11"x26"

3
artist: **SCOTT HAMPTON**
art director: Sue Ann Harkey
client: Magic: The Gathering
title: Skulking Ghost

4
artist: **BROM**
art director: Brom
designer: Brom
client: FPG
title: Blood Ritual
medium: Oil
size: 8"x10"

1

2

3

4

1
artist: **ZOLTAN BOROS**
            & GABOR SZIKSZAI
designer: Zoltan Boros
            & Gabor Szikszai
client: Hungaria Insurance Co.
title: Calendar—Jan./Feb.
medium: Acrylic
size: 14"x10"

2
artist: **ROBERT A. SWEENEY**
art director: Robert A. Sweeney
client: Stanford Telecom
title: Frogger
medium: Acrylic/gouache
size: 36"x30"

3
artist: **KEVIN KRENECK**
art director: Kevin Kreneck
client: The Texas Observer
title: Corporate Rule & Political Puppets
medium: Ink
size: 7"x8"

4
artist: **RAFAL OLBINSKI**
art director: Rita Marshall
designer: Rafal Olbinski
client: Naman Galleries
title: Calendar
medium: Acrylic

1

2

3

4

1
artist: **MIKE DRINENBERG**
art director: Sue Ann Harkey
designer: Visions
client: Magic: The Gathering

2
artist: **TERESE NIELSEN**
art director: Sue Ann Harkey
designer: Sue Ann Harkey
client: Wizards of the Coast
title: Elvish Ranger
medium: Mixed
size: 11″x9″

3
artist: **MICHAEL WHELAN**
client: Self promotion
title: Meditation: The River
medium: Oil on canvas
size: 32″x48″

3

1
artist: **WILL WILSON**
art director: Will Wilson
title: Work In Progress
medium: Oil

2
artist: **PAUL CHADWICK**
art director: Craig Hooper
client: Wizards of the Coast
title: On the Fast Track

3
artist: **MARK COVELL**
designer: Mark Covell
client: Self promotion
medium: Oil
size: 15"x20"

1
artist: **IAN MILLER**
art director: Sue Ann Harkey
client: Magic: The Gathering
title: Aku Dijin
medium: Colored ink

2
artist: **JOHN BOLTON**
art director: Sue Ann Harkey
designer: Sue Ann Harkey
client: Magic: The Gathering
title: Jungle Troll
medium: Mixed

3
artist: **LeUYEN PHAM**
art director: Jim Salvati
designer: LeUyen Pham
client: Self promotion
title: Tales From Poe: Ligeia
medium: Watercolor
size: 5"x10"

4
artist: **PHIL HALE**
art director: Craig Hooper
client: Wizards of the Coast
title: Trouble
medium: Oil

5
artist: **DAVID SEELEY**
art director: Sue Ann Harkey
client: Wizards of the Coast
title: Phyrexian Marauder
medium: Mixed/digital

3

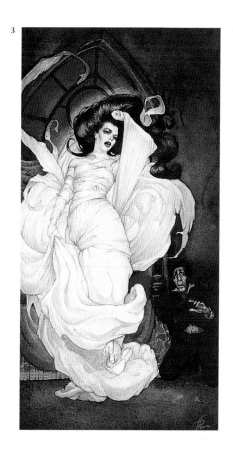

4

5

1
artist: **JON FOSTER**
art director: Jon Foster
client: Self promotion
title: Bee Keeper
medium: Watercolor/digital
size: 4 1/2"x5"

2
artist: **WILLIAM STOUT**
art director: William Stout
designer: William Stout
client: Gameworks
title: Time To Go!
medium: Inks/watercolor/colored
　　　　　pencils on board
size: 18"x14"

3
artist: **JOHN MATSON**
art director: Brom
designer: John Matson
client: FPG
title: True Charisma
medium: Mixed
size: 11 5/8"x15 1/8"

1

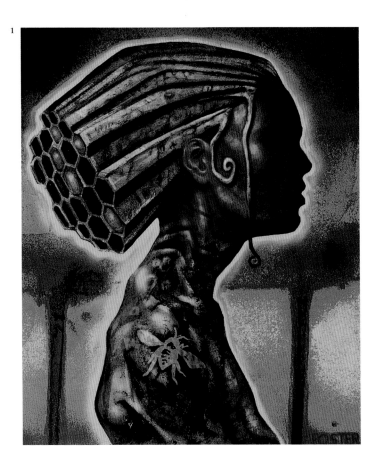

2

artist: **MICHAEL WHELAN**
client: Tree's Place Gallery   *title:* Prudence II   *medium:* Acrylic on hardboard   *size:* 12"x8"

artist: **JEFF MIRACOLA**

designer: Jeff Miracola   *title:* Pray Angel   *medium:* Oil on board   *size:* 11"x14"

1
artist: **PETAR MESELDŽIJA**
art director: Petar Meseldžija
client: Petar Meseldžija
title: A Legend Called Steel-Bashaw
medium: Oil on board
size: 40cmx60cm

2
artist: **SETH ENGSTROM**
title: History of the Future
medium: Acrylic
size: 24"x48"

3
artist: **MARK HARRISON**
art director: Mark Harrison
title: Thailand
medium: Acrylic
size: 23"x13 1/2"

4
artist: **RICHARD HESCOX**
art director: Richard Hescox
designer: Richard Hescox
title: Ancient Memories
medium: Oil on canvas
size: 14"x20"

1

2

3

4

1
artist: **DARREL ANDERSON
   & RICK BERRY**
title: Neo-Zero
medium: Digital

2
artist: **PHIL HALE**
title: Johnny Badhair
medium: Oil

3
artist: **PHIL HALE**
client: FPG
title: #6
medium: Oil

1

2

1
artist: **MICHAEL WHELAN**
title: The Gentle Virtue
medium: Acrylic on watercolor board
size: 13"x11"

2
artist: **MICHAEL DAVID WARD**
art director: Michael David Ward
designer: Michael David Ward
title: Wired
medium: Acrylic on board
size: 20"x30"

3
artist: **JOHN RUSH**
art director: Audrey Niffenegger
client: Shadow Press
title: Study of a Winged Figure
medium: Drypoint
size: 6"x9"

4
artist: **PATRICK KOCHAKJI**
title: Dark Angel
medium: Oil
size: 7"x12 1/2"

4

1
artist: **JOHN W. SLEDD**
art director: John W. Sledd
client: Sledd Studios
title: Outpost At L'Toch Weyr
medium: Digital
size: 9"x7"

2
artist: **FRANÇOIS ESCALMEL**
art director: François Escalmel
title: The Last Supper
medium: Digital

3
artist: **PHIL HALE**
medium: Oil

4
artist: **CHAD DEZERN**
title: Moog Auditorium
medium: Mixed
size: 11"x14"

1

2

3

4

1
artist: **BRIGID MARLIN**
art director: Brigid Marlin
designer: Brigid Marlin
title: Flight of the Churches, Venice
medium: Oil
size: 36"x31"

2
artist: **LeUYEN PHAM**
art director: Robert Rodriguez
designer: LeUyen Pham
title: Evening's Enchantment
medium: Watercolor
size: 10"x15"

3
artist: **SHEILA RAYYAN**
title: Flight of the Churches, Venice
medium: Pencil
size: 4"x7"

4
artist: **MELISSA FERREIRA**
art director: Melissa Ferreira
designer: Melissa Ferreira
title: Buzzworks
medium: Acrylic
size: 10"x14"

1

2

3

1
artist: **YURI BARTOLI**
designer: Yuri Bartoli
title: Young Merlin
medium: Oil
size: 18"x15"

2
artist: **COREY WOLFE**
art director: Corey Wolfe
title: Senders
medium: Oil
size: 32"x32"

3
artist: **ILENE MEYER**
title: Chickiphant
medium: Oil
size: 13"x16"

4
artist: **PETAR MESELDŽIJA**
art director: Petar Meseldžija
client: Petar Meseldžija
title: A Legend Called Steel-Bashaw
medium: Oil on board
size: 40cmx60cm

1

2

3

4

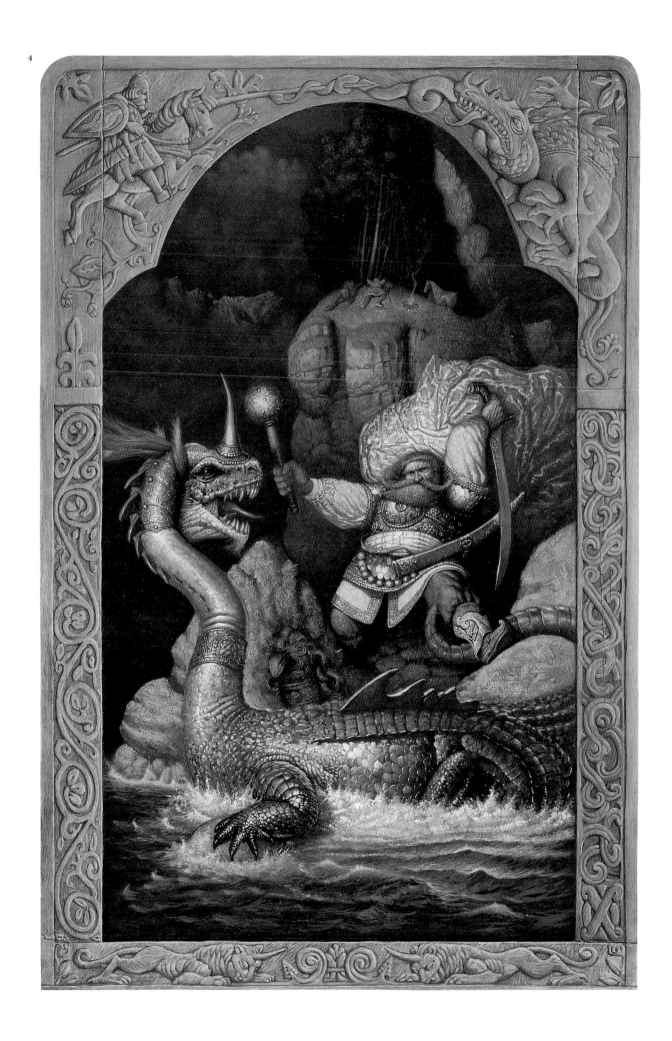

1
artist: **JON SULLIVAN**
art director: Jon Sullivan
title: Tower of Dragons
medium: Oil
size: 10"x21"

2
artist: **EZRA TUCKER**
art director: Ezra Tucker
client: Jack Lew
title: Dragon Kite
medium: Acrylic
size: 36"x60"

3
artist: **BELLA MARSKY**
title: Red Fish
medium: Mixed
size: 24"x12"

4
artist: **ILENE MEYER**
title: Zebrocerous
medium: Oil
size: 16"x13"

5
artist: **DON MAITZ**
art director: Don Maitz
title: Chasing the Wind
medium: Oil
size: 35"x25"

1

2

3

133

1
artist: **STEPHEN HICKMAN**
title: Nagheal the Sorceress
medium: Oil
size: 16"x30"

2
artist: **STEPHAN "CRICKET" MARTINIERE**
title: Blast-Off!
medium: Digital

3
artist: **CARLOS A. BATTS**
art director: Carlos A. Batts
title: Lunar Cycle
medium: Photo/manipulation
size: 11"x14"

4
artist: **TODD LOCKWOOD**
art director: Todd Lockwood
title: Kali
medium: Pencil
size: 17"x22"

1
artist: **CHAD DEZERN**
title: Fat Man/Little Boy
medium: Mixed
size: 14"x11"

2
artist: **PETER KIM**
title: Dropping the Dead
medium: Acrylic
size: 25 1/2"x15"

3
artist: **MARC GABBANA**
title: The General
medium: Acrylic
size: 14"x18"

4
artist: **MICHAEL WHELAN**
title: Prudence
medium: Acrylic on watercolor board
size: 11"x12"

5
artist: **MARC GABBANA**
title: Headin' Home to Hades
medium: Acrylic
size: 18"x10"

1

2

1
artist: **CARL LUNDGREN**
title: Naked Clown
medium: Oil on board
size: 27"x16"

2
artist: **ANITA SMITH**
title: I Gild Thee
medium: Oil
size: 24"x36"

3
artist: **DAVID SEAN SanANGELO**
title: Unity
medium: Oil on board
size: 20"x24"

4
artist: **STU SUCHIT**
art director: John Gibson
designer: John Gibson
title: Angry?
medium: Digital
size: 4½"x7"

1

2

3

1
artist: **PHIL HALE**
medium: Oil on board

2
artist: **PATRICK KOCHAKJI**
title: The Descent of Augustine
medium: Oil
size: 11"x17"

3
artist: **BAGRAM IBATOVLLINE**
title: The Night Watch
medium: Gouache on paper
size: 12"x20"

4
artist: **GREG & TIM HILDEBRANDT**
title: The Queen
medium: Acrylic
size: 19"x31"

4

GREG & TIM
HILDEBRANDT

artist index

Paul Alexander 22, 29
37 Pine Mtn. Rd.
W. Redding, CT 06896
203-544-9293

Darrel Anderson 82,122
1420 Territory Trail
Colorado Springs, CO 80919
719-535-0407

Patrick Arrasmith 8
309 6th St. #3
Brooklyn, NY 11215
718-499-4101

Istvan Banyai 10
c/o Cortez Wells
Playboy Enterprises, Inc.
680 N. Lake Shore Dr.
Chicago, IL 60611

Bryn Barnard 46
432 Point Caution Drive
Friday Harbor, WA 98250
360-378-6355

Yuri Bartoli 80,130
45-21 45th St.
Sunnyside, NY 11104
718-729-0361

Carlos Batts 134
1816 Bolton St. #1
Baltimore, MD 21217
410-225-7671
www.dsp.com/solo/dream

Jill Bauman 16
162-19 65th Ave.
Fresh Meadows, NY 11365
718-886-5616

Sean Beavers 84
c/o Peter Lott Rep.
60 E. 42nd St.
New York, NY 10165
212-953-7088

Doug Beekman 26, 54
31 S. Main #4
Brattleboro, VT 05301

Wes Benscotter 18, 86
1503 Kay St.
Harrisburg, PA 17109

Rick Berry 2, 83, 90, 104, 105, 106
93 Warren St.
Arlington, MA 02174
http://www.braid.com

Guy Billout 10
c/o Cortez Wells
Playboy Enterprises, Inc.
680 N. Lake Shore Dr.
Chicago, IL 60611

Joel Biske 90
159 Avalon Ct.
Roselle, IL 60172
630-894-0269
630-894-0726 [fax]
E/M StudioB159@aol.com

Rob Bliss 100
c/o Sue Ann Harkey
927 22nd Ave.
Seattle, WA 98122
206-328-0612

Richard Bober 87
c/o Jill Bauman
162-19 65th Ave
Fresh Meadows, NY 11365
718-886-5616

John Bolton 114
c/o Liliana Bolton
16-24 Underwood St.
London, N17DQ UK

Zolton Boros 50, 98, 108
c/o Roberto Kohlstedt Rep.
Neue Schule 34
Arenshausen D-37318
Germany

David Bowers 94, 95
206 Arrowhead Ln.
Eighty-Four, PA 15330
419-942-3274

Randy Bowen 70
6803 SE Jack Road
Milwaukie, OR 97222
FAX: 503-786-7948

Eric Bowman 85
7405 SW 154th Pl.
Beaverton, OR 97007
503-644-1016

Jacques Bredy 62
313 W. 17th St.
New York, NY 10011
212-691-9754

Daniel Brereton 50
10281 High St. #A
Truckee, CA 96161
916-546-1259

Brom 90, 97, 107
2470 Huntington Dr.
Pittsburgh, PA 15241

Charles Burns 62
c/o Kitchen Sink Press
320 Riverside Drive
Northampton, MA 01060
413-586-9525

Jim Burns 44
c/o Alan Lynch
11 King's Ridge Rd.
Long Valley, NJ 07853
908-813-8718

Travis Charest 66
c/o Homage Studios
888 Prospect #240
La Jolla, CA 92037

Clyde Caldwell 64
720-A Fox Lane
Waterford, WI 53185
414-534-3313

Paul Chadwick 112
c/o Wizards of the Coast
Craig Hooper
1801 Lind Ave.
Renton, WA 98055

Joe Chiodo 91, 102
8472 Via Sonoma #30
LaJolla, CA 92037

James C. Christensen 21, 30, 47
656 W. 550 S.
Orem, UT 84058

Sean Coons 106
1524 Irving Ave.
Glendall, CA 91201
818-241-7461

Ray-Mel Cornelius 8
1526 Elmwood Blvd.
Dallas, TX 75224
214-946-9405
214-946-5209 [fax]

Mark Covell 113
70 Perkins Rd.
Oxford, CT 06478
203-888-0719

Robert Crumb 24
c/o Kitchen Sink Press
320 Riverside Drive
Northampton, MA 01060
413-586-9525

Geoff Darrow 100
c/o Sue Ann Harkey
927 22nd Ave.
Seattle, WA 98122
206-328-0612

Joseph DeVito 5, 68
1 Holly Court
Flemington, NJ 08822
908-806-4412

Dave DeVries 65, 102
67 Benson Dr.
Wayne, NJ 07470
201-696-3782

Chad M. Dezern 127, 136
14251 Dickens St.
Sherman Oaks, CA 91423
818-553-5121

Tony Diterlizzi 14, 88
405 First St. 2nd Floor
Brooklyn, NY 11215

David Dorman 7
P.O. Box 203
Mary Esther, FL 32579
903-314-1075

Mike Drinenberg 110
c/o Sue Ann Harkey
927 22nd Ave.
Seattle, WA 98122
206-328-0612

Bob Eggleton 52
P.O. Box 5692
Providence, RI 02903
401-738-6281

Tristan A. Elwell 49
c/o Shannon Associates
327 E. 89th St./#3E
New York, NY 10128
212-831-5650

Seth Engstrom 120
120 S. Mentor Ave./#303
Pasadena, CA 91106
818-683-3447

Mike Evans 81
c/o Peter Lott Rep.
60 E. 42nd St.
New York, NY 10165
212-953-7088

François Escalmel 126
2039 Laurier E.
Montreal, Quebec
H2H 1B8 Canada
514-521-8242

Mat Falls 72
31364 Via Colinas #106
Westlake, CA 91362
818-879-1996

Steve Fastner & Rich Larson 63
529 S. 7th St./#445
Minneapolis, MN 55415

Melissa Ferreira 129
231 Nayatt Rd.
Barrington, RI 02806
401-245-8438

Marc Fishman 98
1155 Warburton Ave./11C
Yonkers, NY 10701
914-423-6343

Fred Fields 4, 103
33922 Hillcrest Dr.
Burlington, WI 53105
414-539-3631

Jon Foster 116
231 Nayatt Rd.
Barrington, RI 02806
401-245-8438

Frank Kelly Freas 28
7933 Quimby Ave.
West Hills, CA 91304
818-992-1252

Marc Gabbana 64, 137
2453 Olive Street
Windsor, Ontario
N8T 3N4 Canada
519-948-2418

Nick Gaetano 14
c/o Vicki Morgan Assoc.
194 Third Ave.
New York, NY 10003
212-475-0440
212-353-8538 FAX

Donato Giancola 32, 39, 40
67 Dean St. #3
Brooklyn, NY 11201
718-797-2438

Gnemo 23, 42, 50
c/o Tom Kidd
59 Cross Brook Rd.
New Milford, CT 06776
860-355-1781
E/M tomkidd@spellcaster.com
spellcaster.com/tomkidd

Sergei Goloshapov 24, 30
111 First St./Studio 65E
Jersey City, NJ 07302
201-792-7604

Samuel H. Greenwell 73
105 Copper Field Lane
Georgetown, KY 40324

Rebecca Guay 60
45 Spaulding St.
Amherst, MA 01002
413-253-7999

James Gurney 92
P.O. Box 693
Rhinebeck, NY 12572

Scott Gustafson 89
4045 N. Kostner
Chicago, IL 60641
312-725-8338
312-725-5437 FAX

Phil Hale 78, 96, 104, 115, 122, 123, 126, 140
Unit 26
Spital Square, Spital Fields
London E1 6DX
England

Scott Hampton 106
c/o Sue Ann Harkey
927 22nd Ave.
Seattle, WA 98122
206-328-0612

Joel Harlow 77
10703 1/2 Woodbridge St.
N. Hollywood, CA 91602
818-762-4450

John Harris 22
c/o Alan Lynch
11 King's Ridge Rd.
Long Valley, NJ 07853
908-813-8718

Mark Harrison 120
Flat 3/13 Palmeira Ave.
Hove E. Sussex BN3 3GA
England
01273-739-286

Carol Heyer 35
925 Ave. De Los Arboles
Thousand Oaks, CA 91360

Richard Hescox 121
P.O. Box 50953
Eugene, OR 97405
541-302-9744

Stephen Hickman 42, 45, 134
10 Elm Street
Red Hook, NY 12571

Greg & Tim Hildebrandt 80, 98, 141
c/o Jean L. Scrocco Rep.
120 American Rd.
Morris Plains, NJ 07950
201-292-6854
201-984-6194 [fax]

Brad Holland 3
c/o Cortez Wells
Playboy Enterprises, Inc.
680 N. Lake Shore Dr.
Chicago, IL 60611

Fred Hooper 82
3514 Frontonac Ct.
Aurora, IL 60504
630-851-6914

John Howe 51
c/o Alan Lynch
11 King's Ridge Rd.
Long Valley, NJ 07853
908-813-8718

Bagram Ibatoulline 140
282 Barrow St./1
Jersey City, NJ 07302
201-332-5889

Jael 84
P.O. Box 11178
Fairfield, NJ 07004
973-812-9265

Nicholas Jainschigg 48
12 Campbell St.
Warren, RI 02885
401-245-2954

Bruce Jensen 38
39-39 47th St.
Sunnyside, NY 1104
718-482-9125

Glenn Kim 36
1401 20th Ave./#3
San Francisco, CA 94122

Peter Kim 136
9400 Kramerwood Pl.
Los Angeles, CA 90034
310-838-1958

Patrick Kochakji 125, 140
6820 Shoshone Ave.
Van Nuys, CA 91406
818-343-4144

Joseph Page Kovach 93
1225 Whitney Lane
Westerville, OH 43081
800-355-1647

George Krauter 8
3250 Irving/Apt. 2
San Francisco, CA 94122

Kevin Kreneck 108
1507 Hollywood Ave.
Dallas, TX 75208
214-467-8767

Ray Lago 56, 57
P.O. Box 36
Jersey City, NJ 07303

Jeff Laubenstein 31
2414 N. Newcastle Ave.
Chicago, IL 60707
773-889-1464

Jim Lee 58
c/o Homage Studios
888 Prospect #240
La Jolla, CA 92037

Victor Lee 26, 47
2038 10th Ave.
San Francisco, CA 94116
415-564-2772

Gary A. Lippincott 32
131 Greenville Rd.
Spencer, MA 01562
508-885-9592

Todd Lockwood 135
511 Meado Ave.
Woodstock, IL 60098

Greg Loudon 64
1804 Pine Rd.
Homewood, IL 60430
708-798-5936

Carl Lundgren 138
P.O. Box 825
Lecanto, FL 34460

Don Maitz 27, 35, 133
5824 Bee Ridge Rd./#106
Sarasota, Fl 34233

Brigid Marlin 128
28 Castle Hill
Berkhamsted, Herts
HP4 1HE England
+44-144-286-4454

Bella Marsky 132
111—1st St./#65E
Jersey City, NJ 07302
201-792-7604

Stephan Martiniere 13, 134
818-994-1926

John Matson 117
11215 Research Blvd. #1062
Austin, TX 78759
512-795-2963

Oliver McCrae 76
4508 39th
Lubbock, TX 79414
806-797-4244

Dave McKean 60
c/o Kitchen Sink Press
320 Riverside Drive
Northampton, MA 01060
413-586-9525

Wilson McLean 6
c/o Cortez Wells
Playboy Enterprises, Inc.
680 N. Lake Shore Dr.
Chicago, IL 60611

David W. Meikle 86
1157 Annex/U. of Utah
Salt Lake City, UT 84112
801-585-6883
801-585-6883 [fax]
E/M DAVE@admin.dce.utah.edu

Petar Meseldzua 79, 120, 131
Kogerwatering 49
1541XB Koog A/D Zaan
Nederland
+31-75-6708649

Ilene Meyer 11, 130, 133
c/o Concx International, Inc.
428-No. Rodeo Dr.
Beverly Hills, CA 90210

Ian Miller 114
c/o Worlds of Wonder
P.O. Box 814
McLean, VA 22101
703-847-4251

Lauren Mills 36
106 Nash Hill Rd.
Williamsburge, MA 01096

Jeff Miracola 93, 119
11160 Jollyville Rd. #631
Austin, TX 78759
512-349-7478

Moebius 96
c/o Wizards of the Coast
Craig Hooper
1801 Lind Ave.
Renton, WA 98055

Chris Moore 28, 38
c/o Worlds of Wonder
P.O. Box 814
McLean, VA 22101
703-847-4251

Clayburn Moore 71, 72
11906A Dubloon Cove
Austin, TX 78759
512-219-7297
512-258-2336 [fax]
www.moorecreations.com

Harriett Morton-Becker 70
5537 Old Ranch Rd.
Sarasota, FL 34241
941-924-8245
941-925-7581 [fax]
E/M noctvisn@netline.net

John Mueller 62, 67
c/o Kitchen Sink Press
320 Riverside Drive
Northampton, MA 01060
413-586-9525

James Nelson 42
2011 W. Byron #2
Chicago, IL 60618

Mark Nelson 56
c/o Kitchen Sink Press
320 Riverside Drive
Northampton, MA 01060
413-586-9525

Greg Newbold 84
1231 E. 6600 S.
Salt Lake City, UT 84121
801-268-2209

Terese Nielsen 104, 110
6049 Kauffman Ave.
Temple City, CA 91780

Dennis Nolan 37
106 Nash Hill Rd.
Williamsburge, MA 01096

Rafal Olbinski 12, 15, 17, 109
142 E. 35th St.
New York, NY 10016
212-532-4328

Glen Orbik 66
818-785-7904

James A. Owen 92
P.O. Box 2203
Friday Harbor, WA 98250

John Jude Pallencar 20, 34, 40, 46
249 Elm St.
Oberlin, OH 44074

Paolo Parente 56
Via Trivulzio 30
Milano, Italy 20166
+39-2-6069388

Keith Parkinson 53
c/o Kevin Siembieda
12455 Universal Dr.
Taylor, MI 48180

LeuYen Pham 115, 128
1750 Grevelia St. #1
S. Pasadena, CA 91030
818-403-7006

J.A. Pippett 69
12946 Dikens St.
Studio City, CA 91604

Alan Pollack 52
925 1/2 Dodge St.
Lake Geneva, WI 53147

William Prosser 88
P.O. Box 2591
Yucca Valley, CA 92286
619-365-4547

Omar Rayyan 2
P.O. Box 958
West Tisbury, MA 02575
508-693-5909

Sheila Rayyan 128
P.O. Box 958
West Tisbury, MA 02575
508-693-5909

Romas 33
389 Pako Ave.
Keene, NH 03431
603-357-7306

Alex Ross 61
c/o Homage Studios
888 Prospect #240
La Jolla, CA 92037

Luis Royo 52
c/o Alan Lynch
11 King's Ridge Rd.
Long Valley, NJ 07853
908-813-8718

Steve Rude 58, 59, 60
423 E. Duarte/#C
Arcadia, CA 91006
818-294-0094

Gary Ruddell 32
875 Las Ovejas Ave.
San Rafael, CA 94903

Robh Ruppel 22
1639 Broadview
Glendale, CA 91208
818-249-9341
818-957-7215 [fax]

John Rush 16, 124
123 Kedzie St.
Evanston, IL 60202
847-869-2078

David Sean SanAngelo 138
175 Hinman Lane
Southbury, CT 06488

Marc Sasso 18
4269 Via Marina/#28
Marina Del Rey, CA 90292

Todd Schorr 94, 102
c/o Kitchen Sink Press
320 Riverside Drive
Northampton, MA 01060
413-586-9525

Mark Schultz 55
c/o Kitchen Sink Press
320 Riverside Drive
Northampton, MA 01060
413-586-9525

David Seeley 115
102 South St./#4
Boston, MA 02111
617-423-3195

Wojtek Siudmak 6
c/o Terri Czeczko
9508 Queens Blvd./#6F
Forest Hills, NY 11374

John W. Sledd 126
561 Harris Dr.
Front Royal, VA 22630
800-861-5784

Anita Smith 138
P.O. Box 1195
Tehachapi, CA 93581
714-642-3873

Douglas Smith 48
24 Erie Ave.
Newton, MA 02161
617-558-3256

Lisa Snellings 74
P.O.Box 12323
Augusta, GA 20914
706-738-4132 FAX

John K. Snyder III 25
106 S. Lee St.
Falls Church, Va 22046
703-533-3068

William Stout 19, 116
1468 Loma Vista St.
Pasadena, CA 91104
818-798-6490

Philip Straub 80
50 Laurel Dr.
Monroe, CT 06468
203-261-4334
Rep.: Fran Seigel
212-486-9644

Stu Suchit 4, 139
117 Jayne Ave.
Port Jefferson, NY 11777
516-928-6775

Jon Sullivan 132
18 Highview
75 Eglington Hill
Plumstead, London
SE18 3PB England
+44-0181-316-0367

Robert A. Sweeney 108
3925 Dolphin Circle
Colorado Springs, CO 80918
719-528-5233

Cabor Szikszai 50, 98, 108
c/o Roberto Kohlstedt Rep.
Neue Schule 34
Arenshausen D-37318
Germany

Tom Taggart 75
Kings Village Apt. 314-2
Budd Lake, NJ 07828
201-426-1612

Kerry P. Talbott 4
9740 Candace Terr.
Glen Allen, VA 23060
804-755-5917

Miles Teves 74
1428 Ontario St.
Burbank, CA 91505
818-848-2028

Murray Tinkelman 82
75 Lakeview Ave. W.
Peekskill, NY 10566
914-737-5960

Ezra Tucker 132
P.O. Box 1155
Solvang, CA 93463

Anthony Veilleux 72
50 Ridout St. #20
London, Ontario
Canada N6C 3W6

Ron Walotsky 28
112 Pine Tree St.
Flagler Beach, FL 32136
904-439-1407

Michael David Ward 124
P.O. Box 14396
Santa Rosa, CA 95402
707-585-2329

James Warhola 34
99 Mill St.
Rhinebeck, NY 12572

Brad Weinman 9
5268 Lindley Ave.
Encino, CA 91316

Mark Wheatley 58
7844 St. Thomas Dr.
Baltimore, MD 21236
410-661-6897
410-665-3597 [fax]
E/M insight@clark.net

Michael Whelan 24, 111, 118, 124, 137
P.O. Box 88
Brookfield, CT 06804
203-792-8089

Joe Wilson 101
89 North St.
Hamden, CT 06514
203-776-7690

Will Wilson 112
5511 Knollview Ct.
Balto, MD 21228
410-455-0715

Corey Wolfe 130
18612 NE Risto Rd.
Battleground, WA 98604
360-687-0699

Paul Youll 43
39 Durham Rd.
Esh Winning Co, Durham
DH7 9ND UK

Stephen Youll 41, 44
296 Pegasus Rd.
Piscataway, NJ 08854

John Zeleznik 99
7307 Kelvin #10
Canola Park, CA 91306

This book was set in the Adobe version of the Stone Serif family with handlettering additions.

Spectrum 4 was designed on a Macintosh 7200Power PC.

Book design and handlettering by **Arnie Fenner.**

Art direction and editing by **Cathy Fenner** and **Arnie Fenner.**

Production assistance by **Jim Loehr.**

Printed in Singapore.

ARTISTS, ART DIRECTORS AND PUBLISHERS INTERESTED IN RECEIVING
ENTRY INFORMATION FOR THE NEXT SPECTRUM COMPETITION
should send their name and address to:
Spectrum Design
P.O. Box 4422
Overland Park, KS
66204-0422